MOONLIGHT ENCOUNTER

Carmen studied him in the moonlight, this stranger she had once known so well. He was as beautiful as ever, an Apollo with hair as bright as winter sunlight, tall and elegantly slim. But there was something there that had not been six years ago. Deep lines bracketed his lovely mouth; his eyes were as flat and still as a millpond, no stirring of emotion at seeing her again. It was almost as if another soul had come to inhabit the body of the man she loved.

How could *her* Peter be behind those eyes?

"I thought you dead," she managed to say. "They told me you were killed that day."

The Spanish Bride

Amanda McCabe

A SIGNET BOOK

SIGNET
Published by New American Library, a division of
Penguin Putnam Inc., 375 Hudson Street,
New York, New York 10014, U.S.A.
Penguin Books Ltd, 27 Wrights Lane,
London W8 5TZ, England
Penguin Books Australia Ltd, Ringwood,
Victoria, Australia
Penguin Books Canada Ltd, 10 Alcorn Avenue,
Toronto, Ontario, Canada M4V 3B2
Penguin Books (N.Z.) Ltd, 182–190 Wairau Road,
Auckland 10, New Zealand

Penguin Books Ltd, Registered Offices:
Harmondsworth, Middlesex, England

First published by Signet, an imprint of New American Library,
a division of Penguin Putnam Inc.

First printing, August 2001
10 9 8 7 6 5 4 3 2 1

*To the finest mentors a fledgling writer
could ever ask for—Tori Phillips,
Karen Harbaugh, Linda Castle, and Martha Hix.
I truly could not have done
this without all your help and advice.
Thank you!*

Prologue

"I pronounce you man and wife. In the name of the Father, of the Son, and of the Holy Spirit. Amen."

Carmen Montero, known in her Seville home as the Condesa Carmen Pilar Maria de Santiago y Montero, trembled as the priest made the sign of the cross over her head. Her fingers were chill in her bridegroom's grasp.

It was done. She was married.

Again.

And she had always sworn to herself that she would never again enter the unwelcome bonds of matrimony! She had relished her widowhood, the freedom to live as she pleased, apart from restrictive Seville society. The freedom to work for the cause of ridding Spain of the French interloper.

Her husband, Joaquin, Conde de Santiago, had been good for nothing in life. She shuddered still to think of his cold cruel hands, his rages when, every month, she was *not* pregnant with a son and heir. At least in death his money had proved useful, working to help free Spain from the French.

Yes, she had sworn never to marry again.

Yet she had not foreseen that there could be anything like this man in the world.

When she had first seen Major Lord Peter Everdean, the Earl of Clifton, her heart had skipped a beat, just as in the silly novels her friends had slipped into their convent school so long ago. Then it had leaped to life again. He was just as handsome as she had heard whispered by her friends at balls in Seville, the Ice Earl, as the ladies gigglingly called him.

But it had not been only his golden good looks that drew her. There was something in his beautiful ice-blue eyes: a loneliness, an isolation that she had understood so deeply. It had been what she had felt all her life, this sense of not belonging.

Now perhaps she had found a place she *could* belong, even in the midst of war. Perhaps they both had.

Carmen peeked up through her lashes at the man beside her, only to find him watching her intently, a faint smile on his lips.

She smiled slowly in return, once she could catch her breath. The only word that could describe Peter was *beautiful*. He was as elegant and golden as an archangel, his fair hair and sun-bronzed skin gleaming in the candlelight of the small church. His broad shoulders gave a muscular contour to his red coat and his impossibly lean hips looked charming in tight-fitting white pantaloons. His rare smiles enticed women the entire length of Andalucia, and every place he went.

Now his ring was on *her* finger. Tall, skinny, bookish Carmen. This extraordinary man was her husband, her lover, even her friend.

It was all suddenly overwhelming, the incense in the church, the emotions in her heart. She swayed precariously, only to be caught in her husband's strong arms.

"Carmen!" he said. "What is it?"

"I just need some fresh air," she whispered.

Nicholas Hollingsworth, Peter's fellow officer and their only witness, hurried down the aisle ahead of them to throw open the carved doors. "She is probably exhausted, Peter," He pointed out. "She rode all day to get here!"

"Yes," Carmen agreed. "I am just a bit tired. But the air is a great help."

Indeed it was. Her head was clearer already, in the cool, dry night. She leaned her forehead against her husband's shoulder and closed her eyes, breathing deeply of his heady scent of wool, leather, and sandalwood soap.

"I am a brute," he murmured against her hair. "You should have been asleep these many hours, and here I have insisted on dragging you before the priest."

Carmen laughed. "Oh, I do not think I mind so very much."

"It was past time for the two of you to make it respectable," Nicholas said. "You have been making calves' eyes at each other for weeks, every time Carmen comes into camp. It was quite the scandal."

"Untrue!" Carmen cried, laughing. "You are the scandal, Nick, chasing all the *señoritas* in the village."

"I do not have to chase them! I stand still and they come to me." Nicholas saluted them smartly, and turned to make his way back down the hill to the lights of the British encampment. "Good night, Lord and Lady Clifton!"

Carmen and Peter watched him go, silent together in the warm, starlit night, and in the sense of the profundity of the step they had just taken.

They had known each other only about two months, in intermittent visits Carmen made to the various encampments of Peter's regiment. Yet Carmen had somehow *known,* the moment she had seen him, that he was quite special.

"I remember when I first saw you," she said.

"Do you?"

"Yes. The day I rode in from Seville to speak to Colonel Smith-Mason. You were playing cards with Nicholas outside your tent, in just your shirtsleeves. Most improper. The sun was shining in your hair, and you were laughing. You were quite the most handsome thing I had ever seen."

"I also remember that day. You were riding hell-for-leather through the camp, on that demon you call your horse. You were wearing trousers and that ridiculous hat you love so much." He laughed. "I had never seen a woman like you."

"Hmph, thank you *very* much! I will have you know that that hat is the height of fashion right now."

"I stand corrected, Condesa. But I could not believe that anyone so very lovely, so refined, could be a spy."

"I am not a spy," she corrected him. "I simply sometimes overhear useful information that could perhaps aid you in ridding my country of this French infestation."

"So that is not spying."

"No. It is—helping."

Peter laughed, the rumble of it warm against her. "Then, I am very glad indeed that you have decided to help *us.* You, my dear, could be a formidable foe."

"Not as formidable as you." Carmen fell silent, turning her new ring in the moonlight to admire the flash of the single, square-cut emerald. Peter had told her that the ring had been his mother's, who had died when he was a small child. "This war cannot go on forever."

"No." Peter's hand covered hers, tracing the ring

with his thumb. "Are you sorry now, Carmen, that we married so hastily? Are you having second thoughts about sharing your life with mine after the war?"

"No! Are you?"

"Of course not. You are the only woman I have ever loved."

Carmen's brow arched doubtfully. "Really?"

His laugh was rueful. "I did not say the only woman I have ever *known*. You would see that for a sham immediately. But you are the only woman I have ever loved."

"Then, you did not ask me to marry you out of some sense of obligation, after—well, after what occurred last week?"

"Are you referring to the fact that we anticipated our wedding vows?" Peter clicked his tongue. "My dear, how indelicate!"

Carmen couldn't help but blush just a bit at the memory of that night, when, tipsy with brandy and kisses and a dance beside a river, they had fallen into his bed and done such incredibly wonderful, wicked things. Peter's hands, his sorcerer's mouth . . .

A giggle escaped.

"No," Peter continued. "I married you because I think it is so charming that, despite the fact that you can ride and shoot like the veriest rifle sergeant, you still blush at the mention of the, ah, small preview of our marital bed."

"Small, *querido*?"

"Well, perhaps not *so* small."

"No." Carmen smiled. "Yet have you thought of after the war, when we must leave here and go to England, and you must present me as your countess?"

"Of course I have thought of it! It is almost all I do when we are apart. It will be wonderful. I have a sister and an estate that I have neglected these many years, so we must go there as soon as we can."

"You have been doing your duty for your country 'these many years.' Surely your family must understand that?"

"Yes, but it does not make it any easier to be parted from them. Sometimes, when I cannot sleep at night, I think of them, Elizabeth and Clifton Manor. I can almost smell the green English rain . . ." His voice trailed faintly away.

Carmen looked out over the lights of the camp. She had never been to England, or indeed anywhere but Spain. It was all she knew, warm, sunny, tradition-bound Spain. How would she fare in a new, English life?

She leaned her head against his shoulder, her eyes tightly shut. "Will they like me at your home? Will your sister like me?"

Peter tipped her chin up with one long finger, forcing her to meet his gaze. "Elizabeth will love you; you are very much like her. They will all love you at Clifton. As I do. Believe me, darling, it is much easier to be an English countess than a Spanish one, and you have done that wonderfully. You must not be afraid."

Her jaw tightened. "I am not afraid."

Peter laughed "Excellent! I knew that a woman who does the things you do could not possibly be frightened of the English *ton*." He kissed her lightly on her nose. "Are you ready to return to camp?"

"Oh, yes."

The encampment was uncharacteristically quiet as they made their way hand in hand to Peter's tent. A few groups of men played desultory games of cards around the fires. Outside the largest tent, Colonel Smith-Mason stood with some of his officers, talking in low voices over a sheaf of dispatches.

Peter glanced at them with a small frown.

"Do you think there is something amiss?" Carmen whispered. She had lived long enough with the intrigues of war to know that events could change in an instant, but she had hoped, prayed, that her wedding night at least could prove uneventful.

Outside the bedchamber, anyway.

"I do not know," Peter answered, his watchful gaze still on the small group. "Surely not."

"But you do not *know*?"

He shrugged, "We have more important things to think of tonight," he said, bending his head to softly kiss her ear.

Carmen shivered, but waved him away. "No, you must find out. I will wait."

"Are you certain?"

"Yes. Go on. We have many hours before dawn." He kissed her again, and she watched him walk away, his polished buttons gleaming in the firelight. Then she turned to duck into his tent. *Their* tent, for that night.

It was a goodly size, but almost spartan in its tidiness. The cot was made up with linen-cased pillows and a blue woolen blanket; a stack of papers and books was lined up exactly on the table, and the chairs pushed in at precise angles. His shaving kit and monogrammed ivory hairbrush were flush with his small shaving mirror. The only bit of personal expression was in the miniature portrait on a small stand beside the cot: of his younger sister, Elizabeth. Next to it was a portrait of Carmen, painted when she was 16, which she had given him as a wedding gift.

Carmen laid her small bouquet of wild red roses beside the paintings and went to open her own small trunk, which had been brought there while they were at the church. In it were the only things she had brought away on her journey from Seville: two muslin dresses and a satin gown, a pair of boots, rosary beads, men's trousers and shirts, and a cotton nightrail that was far too practical for a wedding night.

She slipped out of her simple white muslin wedding dress, and took the high ivory comb and white lace mantilla from her hair. She brushed out her waist-length black hair. Then she sat down on the cot to wait.

She was quite asleep when she at last felt Peter's kiss on her cheek, his hand on her back, warm through her silk chemise. She blinked up at him and smiled. "What was it?"

"It is nothing." He sat down beside her and gathered her into his arms. He had shed his coat and shirt, and Carmen rubbed her cheek against the golden satin of his skin. "There were rumors of a French regiment nearby, much closer than they should be."

"Only rumors?"

"Yes. For tonight." He wrapped his fingers in her loose hair and tilted her face up to his, trailing small, soft kisses along the line of her throat. "Tonight is only ours, my wife."

"Oh, yes. My husband. *Mi esposo*." Carmen moaned as his mouth found the crest of her breast through the silk. Her fingernails dug into his bare shoulders. "Only ours."

The bridal couple was torn from blissful sleep near dawn by the horrifying sounds of gunfire, panicked shouts, and braying horses.

Peter was out of bed in an instant, pulling on his uniform as he threw back the tent flaps.

Carmen stumbled after him in bewilderment, drawing the sheet around her naked shoulders. "What is it?" she cried. "A battle?"

"Stay here!" Peter ordered. Then she was alone.

Carmen hastily donned her shirt and trousers, and tied her hair back with a scarf. She was searching for her boots when she heard her husband's voice and that of Lieutenant Robert Means, a young man she had sometimes played cards with of a quiet evening. And fleeced regularly.

"By damn!" Peter cursed. "How could they be so close? How could they have gotten so far without us knowing?"

"Someone must have informed them," Robert answered. "But we are marching out within the quarter hour."

"Of course. I shall be ready. Has Captain Hollingsworth been alerted?"

"Yes. What of . . ." Robert's voice lowered. "What of your wife, Major?"

"I will see to her."

Carmen stuck her head outside the tent. "She will see to herself, thank you very much! And what are you doing running about unarmed, *husband*?" She rattled his saber at him.

"Carmen!" Peter pushed her back into the tent. "You must ride into the hills and wait. I will send an escort with you."

"Certainly not! You require every man. I have ridden about the country without an escort for months. Shall I ride to General Morecambe's encampment and tell him you require reinforcements?"

"No! You are to find a safe place, and wait there until I come for you."

"*Madre de Dios!*" Carmen pulled her leather jacket out of her trunk and thrust her arms into the sleeves, glaring at him all the while. "I will not hide! I cannot play the coward now. I will ride for reinforcements."

"Carmen! Be sensible!"

"You be sensible, Peter! I have been doing this sort of thing for a long time."

"But you were not my wife then!" he shouted.

"Ah. So that is it." Carmen left off loading her pistol to go to him, and framed his handsome, beloved face in her hands. "I cannot give up what I am doing to become a fine, frail, sheltered lady again, simply because I am now your wife. No more than you can stay safely here in camp because you are now my husband."

He turned his head to kiss her palm. "No. Even though I wish it so, you are quite right."

"We shall have many, many years to sit calmly by the fire, *querido*."

He smiled against her skin. "And will you long for your grand adventures, Carmen, when you are chasing babies about Clifton Manor?"

"Never!"

Peter caught her against him and kissed her mouth, hard, desperate. "I will see you at supper, then, Lady Clifton."

"Yes." Carmen clung to him for an instant, an eternal moment, then stepped away. "Promise me you will fight very, very carefully today, Peter."

"Of course, my love." He grinned at her, the white, crooked grin that had won her heart. "I never fight any other way."

Then he was gone.

The men had been gone for almost a half hour when Carmen rode out for the hills, set on her task.

She did not even see the glint of the sun on the rifle barrel as it aimed through the trees. She heard nothing, until the bullet shot from the barrel and landed in her shoulder.

The force of the shot knocked her from her horse, and she lay there in the dust, too stunned to feel pain.

She reached her fingers slowly to touch her shoulder. They came away a bright, sticky red.

"Is this it, then?" she whispered. "*Madre de Dios,* how can I die now?"

Her vision was very blurred when a face swam into view. A broad, sun-burned face, with drooping mustaches and deceptively merry blue eyes. A face she recognized from balls and receptions in Seville, where she danced with French officers and sometimes ferreted secrets from them.

"Well, well, *señora!*" he said. "Or should I say, *Madame la Condesa?* You must allow me to offer my best wishes on your nuptials."

"Chauvin," she whispered.

"Ah, so you are conscious? *Très bein!* You have been plaguing my regiment for weeks, you and your friends the so-called partisans. Now it is my turn, *Madame la Condesa.* There are some small questions I would like to ask you."

"I won't . . . tell you anything," she managed to croak through her parched throat.

"*Au contraire, ma belle chère.* I think you will. But back at my lodgings, where we can speak—comfortably. After I have a glimpse of the little battle that is taking shape. Perhaps we will even see your new husband there!"

Major Chauvin slid his arms none too gently beneath Carmen and pulled her to her feet.

Not surprisingly, she fainted quite away.

"*Nicholas!*" Peter shouted out, unheard over the infernal din of battle, as he watched his friend fall beneath a rifle shot, facedown in the mud and muck.

He fought his way to him, slashing out like a madman at any who dared get in his way. When he at last reached Nicholas, Peter hoisted him onto his shoulder and dragged him out of the very thick of the fighting.

"Hot fighting today, eh, Peter?" Nicholas gasped, choking blood onto the sleeve of Peter's already ruined uniform.

"For God's sake, man, don't talk!"

"Am I . . . done for?"

"Not if I can help it." Peter squinted through the smoke and dust. "Where is the damned field hospital?"

"North of here." Robert Means had appeared beside them, his red hair quite black with gunpowder and mud. "Is he badly off?"

"Bad enough." Peter looked down at Nicholas, who was now slumped in a stupor. "But he can live if I get him to a surgeon soon."

"I'll help you." Robert slipped Nicholas's other arm over his shoulder, and looked about to take their direction. "Bloody hell!"

"What now?"

"Look!"

Peter followed the line of Robert's pointing finger, and saw Major Francois Chauvin, the French leader they had been parrying with and retreating from for months. He was mounted, and his horse was climbing swiftly into the hills above the heat of the fighting. Perched before him, cradled in his arms, loverlike, was a woman.

Even from this distance, Peter could recognize the banner of black satin hair. The hair that had been spread across his pillows only that morning.

It was Carmen in the Frenchman's arms, Peter's one-day wife.

"Ah, *ma chère.* How very thirsty you look, how very much in pain," Chauvin cooed. He poured himself a glass of water from an earthenware pitcher and sipped at it, his cool, hawk-like eyes never leaving Carmen. "It would be so very much easier on you *and* me if you would simply tell me what I must know. Then I could summon the physician, who could give you laudanum. Please, *ma belle*, let me help you."

Carmen, slumped in a straight-backed wooden chair, was almost unconscious from the burning, sticky pain that shot from her shoulder down her entire body. She tasted blood from where Chauvin had struck her repeatedly across the face. She ached for water.

Still, she shook her head.

Chauvin clicked his tongue chidingly. "I was so very afraid you would do that. You Spanish are so very stubborn." He reached for her hand, cradling it on his soft, repulsively moist palm.

One of his fingers trailed over her ring, the emerald Peter had placed there only the night before.

The night before? It seemed a lifetime, an eternity ago.

"Ah," said Chauvin, his hand tightening on hers until she heard the bones grind. "It is the English major who is causing these silly scruples, is it not?"

Carmen just stared at him.

"Yes. Well, *ma chère*, there is no need. The English, he is surely dead by now, and if he is not, he will soon hear of his bride's dreadful perfidy. The jealous one will take care of that for me." He slid the ring onto his own smallest finger. "You will not be needing this anymore, *ma belle*. Madame Chauvin in Paris will be amused by it when I send it to her."

The pain, the gnawing pain, of her wound grew faint as she looked at her wedding ring, Peter's mother's ring, on the fat finger of that French pig. Instead, a rage flared in her heart unlike any she had ever known. Now strength flowed through her, fueled by this white-hot anger. She sat up straighter, her arm cradled against her abdomen.

Then Chauvin made his great mistake.

He half turned away from her to pour another glass of water. His gaze was cast down to the pitcher.

And his sidearm was toward her.

Without thought, Carmen lunged forward and seized the pistol. In one quick, smooth movement, she pulled it up out of the holster, cocked it, and fired it into his heart.

Chauvin fell at her feet, only able to gasp once, his eyes sightless even as they found her pale face, the gun in her hand.

Then he was dead.

She stared down at him for one endless instant, at the blood trickling from his mouth, seeping from his wound. She knelt beside him carefully, and yanked her ring off his finger.

Only when it was safely back where Peter had placed it did all the pain and the fear rush back onto her. She fell back heavily against the chair leg, gasping for breath.

Chauvin was dead, but her troubles were only beginning. Surely someone else in the French encampment had heard the shot; any moment now they would burst through the door, and she would be dead.

Never to see Peter, or hear his voice, or feel his kisses on her skin again.

Still clutching the pistol, Carmen hauled herself to her feet and made her way across the room to the single, high window. It was large enough for her to fit through, if she could only pull herself up to it.

Her shirt was soaked through with sweat and blood by the time she managed to drag a chair beneath the window, climb up on it, and pull herself through the casement. She collapsed from the intense pain when she hit the hard-packed ground, but soon revived.

And began to make her slow, painful way down the hill . . .

A month after the battle, Peter was set to becoming very foxed indeed.

But not quite foxed enough yet. He still saw Carmen in his mind, beautiful and radiant at their wedding; leaning limp against the shoulder of that French pig Chauvin.

He still heard the voice of the Spanish partisan, telling him what he had heard of Carmen's death.

Peter reached for the half-empty bottle of cheap, raw whiskey and, ignoring the rather dingy glass, poured a measure of it straight from the bottle down his throat.

He threw back his head and closed his eyes against the sharp sting of the alcohol. It seemed to him, in his hazy state, that perhaps when he opened his eyes she would be there, sitting across from him, her booted feet propped on the scarred table. Laughing at him, for believing she, the most *alive* person he had ever seen, could be dead.

But when he opened them, there was only the dank *taverna*, crowded with English soldiers waiting for their passage home, rough Spanish sailors, and dark tavern maids in low-cut blouses.

A few of them had already expressed interest in Peter, but he had rebuffed them. There could be solace in the sex act, of course, but now he preferred to find it in a bottle. None of these women had Carmen's elegance, the sharp intelligence that lit her dark eyes, the fine grain of her skin.

None of them *were* Carmen.

He took another pull on the whiskey bottle, and wiped his mouth on the back of his wrist. When he looked up, he saw Robert Means, his arm in a sling, standing in the doorway, looking about the crowded room.

Peter feared he knew what Robert was looking for, and he was right. When Robert's eyes lit on Peter's corner table, he nodded and crossed the room. It took him quite a while, as he had to thread his way through the packed masses of people. Peter debated fleeing while he had the chance, ducking out of the back door; he had no desire to see or speak to anyone.

But he feared his reflexes were too dulled by the whiskey, and he could only sit and watch as Robert reached his table and sat down in the chair across from him. The chair where Peter had imagined Carmen sitting.

"You were meant to be aboard ship an hour ago. We sail at dawn," said Robert. "I said that I would find you before then and bring you back."

Peter shrugged. "Why don't you just sail without me?"

"Are you saying you do not want to return to England?" Robert's tone was deeply shocked. "You wish to stay here?"

"Why not? Here is good. Here is fine. Better than England, anyway. I can't face them there, their pitying glances and their curious questions."

"What would I tell Lady Elizabeth? That I abandoned you in some dockside taverna?"

"Tell my sister any damn thing you want. She's better off without me, in this sorry condition." He took another long drink from the bottle, and held it out to Robert. "D'you want some?"

Robert shook his head, but he took the bottle out of Peter's hand and examined it. "Did you drink all of this yourself?"

"Of course."

"Oh, Peter. I have never known you to lose control in such a manner," Robert placed the bottle at the edge of the table, away from the reach of Peter's grasp. "She is not worth it."

"What? My wife is dead, and it is not worth my becoming disguised?"

"You saw her, Peter! With Chauvin."

Peter shrugged. "What does that signify? It could have been any number of things. Chauvin could have raided our camp . . ."

Robert shook his head and looked away. A faint blush stained the sun-weathered skin of his cheeks. "Oh, my friend."

"What are you shaking your head dolefully about?"

"I did not want to tell you this, not with all that has happened." Robert's voice was low and mournful. "A friend would not add to your grief so."

A cold pit of ice formed low in Peter's stomach; an ice that not even cheap whiskey could melt. "What do you mean, Robert? I could scarce be any lower than I am now. So tell me whatever it is. You are plainly longing to unburden yourself."

Robert nervously licked his lower lip; his hands folded and unfolded on the table. "I did hear, when I was in Seville, that—that . . ."

Peter had never been a patient man. In his cups, he was even less so. He slapped the flat of his hand against the table. "By damn, Robert, say it this instant or shut up!"

Robert looked directly at Peter then, his eyes wide, sad, and guileless. "I heard in Seville that Carmen and Chauvin had been—lovers."

The ice spread at those words, touching Peter's heart. When he was able to speak, the words came out thick and strangled. "What nonsense! I am sure

that she gave the impression of flirtatiousness with
him at the balls there. That was part of her work.
But she would never have shared his bed."

Robert's gaze dropped. "I fear she shared more
than his bed."

"What do you mean?"

"She shared secrets. *Our* secrets, English secrets.
That is why Chauvin knew of our troop movements
at Alvaro."

Without warning, a fire flickered through Peter,
melting the numbness of the ice and leaving a blinding fury. Peter lunged across the table and caught
Robert by the front of his coat, half pulling him from
the chair. "By God, man, if you are lying to me . . ."

Robert shook his head fiercely. "I vow to you,
Peter, on my mother's life, I am not lying! I heard it
from Carmen's best friend, Elena Granjero. She has
known Carmen since she was a child. She vowed to
me that this was the truth, that she could no longer
conceal it now that—that Carmen is gone. Carmen
was a French spy!"

Peter slowly released Robert and fell back into his
chair. Then, all at once, the grief, the whiskey, the
betrayal were all far too much for him. He buried
his face in his hands and wept.

It was a pale, thin wraith of a man who stepped
from the ship at Dover. His uniform sagged off his
shoulders, and his overlong golden hair flopped
across his brow and over his collar.

His sister Elizabeth, though, did not hesitate for a
moment. She raced along the dock, her blue cloak
flying behind her, and flung her arms around his
neck.

"Peter!" she sobbed, her tears wet against his neck.
"Oh, Peter, I feared I would never see you again! It

has been so very long, and you have not written me in ages."

"So very long." Peter held her to him very tightly, his cheek against the dark swirls of her hair. Then he set her gently aside. "Oh, don't fuss so, Lizzie! I am here now, am I not? Whatever passed before is of little moment."

He turned away from her, and walked away to where their carriage waited, the Everdean crest gleaming gilt-edged in the sunlight. He climbed inside without a backward glance.

Elizabeth turned her bewildered gaze to Peter's companion. Robert Means shook his head sadly, and smiled at her.

"I fear, Lady Elizabeth," he said quietly, "that your brother has had quite a dreadful shock."

Far away, a baby was taking her first breath, filling her tiny lungs and sending a piercing shriek out into the world.

"It is a girl, Condesa!" The midwife placed the squirming new bundle of humanity on her mother's chest. "A beautiful girl."

Esperanza Martinez, Carmen's duenna since her childhood, leaned over to peer into the baby's face, now as wrinkled as her own. "What shall you name her, Carmencita?"

Carmen, exhausted and exultant, wrapped her arms about her new daughter's slippery body and held her against her breast. "I shall call her Isabella. After my mother."

Esperanza nodded. "That is a very good name."

Carmen looked down at Isabella. She could see that her features, though rather squashed at the moment, were fine and lovely. The fingers that curled around her own were long and elegant.

Just like her father's.

Carmen began to cry then, great, large tears that spilled from her cheeks and splashed onto the baby. "Oh!" she sobbed. "If only her papa could see her."

Esperanza's thin mouth twisted. "Yes. If only."

Chapter One

England—Six years later

"Shall we see London very soon, Carmencita?"
The Condesa Carmen Pilar Maria de Santiago y Montero smiled across the carriage at her companion. Esperanza Martinez appeared distinctly green about the edges after all the miles of rough roads they had been obliged to endure. Carmen herself was completely convinced that her bruised nether regions would never be quite the same again.

"Very soon, I am sure," she answered. "You will see the fabled golden spires of London, never fear, Esperanza!"

"Really, Mama?" Isabella de Santiago, who had been very quiet for a six-year-old on their grueling journey, looked up from her doll with a glint in her dark eyes. "Are the spires *really* golden?"

"No doubt, Bella. And streets paved with rubies, just like that book about England we have been reading," Carmen said with a laugh.

Esperanza briefly lowered her handkerchief from her mouth and said, "Your mother is telling you what these English call a 'Banbury tale,' Isabella *niña*. London is no more paved with rubies than Seville or Vienna or Paris was. And it is probably a good deal dirtier."

Carmen shrugged. "Where did you hear such a phrase as 'Banbury tale,' Esperanza? I vow you have been reading those Minerva Press novels again. I knew that those packages from your friend Señora Benitez in London were horrid novels!"

"No such thing!" Esperanza surreptitiously tucked *Lady Arabella's Curse* deeper into her reticule.

Isabella had heard little past the word "dirty." Her tiny nose wrinkled. "It could never be as dirty as Paris!"

"Oh, *querida*," Carmen murmured, putting her arm around her daughter's shoulders. "You liked living in Paris, did you not?"

Isabella thought this over very carefully. "I liked our house, and the carousel in the park. And Monsieur Danet's sweetshop. He always gave me extra *raisins glace*, because they were my favorites."

Esperanza's lips pursed at the memory of smears on dainty white frocks. She loved order and properness above all, and unfortunately Carmen and Isabella were not the sorts to always live by those precepts.

"But it was very dirty," Isabella concluded.

"Well, London will surely be no dirtier than Paris," said Carmen. "And I am certain that you will like our new house, Isabella. The estate agent says there is a small park right across the square, and Esperanza and I will even take you to have ices at Gunter's, and to Astley's Amphitheater. If you are very, very good."

"What is an Astley's, Mama?"

"Come and lay your head on Mama's lap, and she will tell you all about the acrobats and trained bears at Astley's."

Minutes later, lulled by the motion of the carriage and the soft sound of her mother's voice, Isabella was fast asleep, her rosebud mouth open against Carmen's red velvet cloak. Even Esperanza was snoring softly.

Carmen leaned her head back against the leather squabs, and finally let her smile slip away. It *had* been a long and arduous journey, and it was far from over. It would not be over even when they reached London. Not for her.

They had not left Paris only for a change of society, as she had told Esperanza when she had asked her to pack their trunks yet again. The fortune she had inherited from her mother's family, along with the annuity from her first late husband, was vast, and they could have gone anywhere—Rome, Venice, Baden-Baden.

Anywhere but the one country Carmen had so carefully avoided on all their ceaseless travels.

If not for those letters . . .

She reached into her own reticule and drew out the cheap envelope, grubby and creased, sealed with sinister-looking black wax. She knew the words by rote now, the ugly words, but she unfolded it and read it again:

"If you have no desire for your own, treacherous role in the occurrences of September 1811 . . . Alvaro Hill . . . the deaths of so many fine Englishmen . . . treacherous spies . . . send five hundred pounds to the address which will soon be revealed to you, Countess Shadow."

"Shadow" had been her name on the dispatches of long-ago days, days of great secrecy and danger in Spain. No one could know of that now, or know of that awful day when she had lost her whole world with the speed of a bullet.

No one but this person. This person who sent her nasty letters from England.

She shoved the letter back into her reticule with a whispered curse. There had been three such missives coming to the house in Paris, each becoming nastier as she refused to capitulate. She had nothing to fear from any revelations of her life in wartime Spain. She had only done what she had to do. But a scandal on Isabella's head, when Carmen had worked so very hard to build a place in Society for her, would be unbearable.

Carmen had only the best planned for her little girl. The best schools, the best tutors, the finest marriage. A duke at the very least! Perhaps a prince. It was only fitting for *her* daughter.

Carmen had her own way of dealing with offal that threatened Isabella's golden future. It had to be someone who had known her in Spain, perhaps a member of Peter's regiment. If any of them had survived. When she found this letter writer, he would be very sorry indeed.

But, oh! To go to England!

Her nerves had been on edge ever since their ship reached the English shore. It had been just as she feared. She saw *him* in every red coat, heard him in every aristocratic accent.

Over the years, she had dashed across the Continent so fast that she had almost outrun the sound of an indifferent voice saying, "What, that blond bloke? He's dead, he is. Died back at Alvaro. Din't you hear?"

Dead. Her Peter, her husband, was dead.

Yet he was not truly dead. Not in her heart, not in their child.

Carmen's hand smoothed over her daughter's guinea-gold curls, pushing them back from her small face. Isabella felt so tiny against her, so vulnerable.

"Oh, Peter," Carmen whispered. "If only you were here. I am so tired, I do not know how much longer I can do everything by myself. If only . . ."

But Carmen knew all too well the horrible futility of "if only."

Chapter Two

"Shall I lay out your blue coat for the evening, my lord?"

Peter Everdean, the Earl of Clifton, sat staring down at the papers on his desk, ostensibly reading them. In reality, he had not seen a word in fully fifteen minutes, or heard anything that Simmons, his valet, had said.

He had been contemplating the offer of marriage he was thinking of making to Lady Deidra Clearbridge, a very suitable, pretty, accomplished, and (it had to be confessed) rather dull young lady of good family.

"Hm?" he murmured. "Blue coat?"

"Yes, my lord."

"Why the deuce would I need my blue coat?" He tugged absently at his rather disheveled cravat, which had, only that morning, been a perfectly executed Mathematical. "I am quite well dressed enough at the moment for an evening at home."

"Yes, my lord. Quite." Simmons looked down his rather long nose at the rumpled cravat and shirtsleeves. His lordship's clothes *did* tend rather to wrinkle when he was going over estate business. "However, it was my understanding that Lady Elizabeth arrives this afternoon from Italy, and that she has sent word she wishes to attend the Duchess of Dacey's ball this evening."

Peter looked up at that, his ice-blue eyes almost horrified behind his spectacles. "Elizabeth! By Jove, I had quite forgotten all about her arrival. No one but my sister would ever wish to attend a confounded crush like the Dacey ball after a grueling journey from Venice."

"Yes, my lord. So—the blue coat?"

"Yes, yes, the blue coat. And quickly, man! She could be here at any moment." The sun was setting beyond his library windows even as they spoke.

Simmons bowed and retreated.

Peter cursed again, and tore off his spectacles. He loved his sister, and of course the house was a great deal livelier when she and her crowd of artistic friends and admirers were about. But she felt that when she was in London, she had to attend every rout, every musicale, every ball, every tea in order to find clients and further her promising career as a portrait painter. It was the only reason, she said, to ever leave her sunny Italian home for the gloominess of London.

And, more often than not, Peter's old friend, Sir Nicholas Hollingsworth, would find a way to wriggle out of escorting her and she would insist on dragging Peter along behind her. What was worse, she insisted on introducing him to every pretty, unmarried girl she could find. This was a severe disruption of his purposely quiet life, filled with political discussions at his club, meetings at the House of Lords (when in session) a few respectable parties with serious-minded people, Lady Deidra by his side . . . perhaps a cozy evening or two with Yvette, until their association had come to its recent end.

Peter called his life quite satisfactory, peaceful, and quiet after years at war. Elizabeth called it an early crypt, and saw it as her bounden duty to get him out into the world again.

He sighed, and shoved his spectacles and account books into a drawer. He would just have to resign himself to the social whirl for the next few weeks. And perhaps Elizabeth was correct in her opinions; he *had* played the mourning recluse, the wounded war hero, for too long. It had been six years since he had been invalided home to England; his melancholy, his "spells," had been a very convenient excuse not to live since then. It hurt far less that way.

Well, Elizabeth would surely be happy to hear of his intentions toward Lady Deidra.

"Isabella? Isabella, *querida*, wake up. We are here. Home." Carmen lifted her daughter's sleepy weight against her shoulder. "Can you walk?"

"No." Isabella buried her nose against the fur collar of her mother's cloak.

"Then, I shall have to carry you, even though you are almost too big and heavy for your mama!" Carmen hoisted her high in her arms and stepped down from the carriage.

The house, a narrow, respectable, cream-colored stone on a well-kept square, was shuttered and quiet as Carmen made her way up the scrubbed marble steps. Esperanza hurried before her to unlock the door.

Late afternoon sunlight streamed from the high windows of the small foyer, revealing furniture still shrouded in holland covers. The butler, housemaid, and cook were not engaged to start until the next day, though there were signs that someone had been in to clean for them.

One round, gilded table was uncovered and held a silver tray piled high with cards.

"Look, Carmen!" Esperanza whispered excitedly as she sifted through them. "Look at all the invitations that have already arrived."

"That is most gratifying, Esperanza, but I absolutely must put this child down before I peruse them. My arm is quite numb."

"Oh, Carmen, give her to me! I will find her bedroom."

"Excellent. *Gracias*, Esperanza." Carmen surrendered her daughter's weight with a grateful sigh. "Do you suppose there might be some tea to be had?"

"I will look. A pot of tea would be most soothing." Then Esperanza carried Isabella up the narrow staircase, crooning to her a soft Spanish lullaby, which she had once sung to Carmen as a child.

Carmen unpinned her small fur hat and ruffled her cropped black curls wearily. She sorted through the invitations, mostly from people she had met on her travels and who had known of her arrival in London, without a great deal of interest.

It *was* gratifying that there were so many of them. Her quiet demeanor, her natural sense of reserve, had quite unwittingly created an aura of mystery and elegance about her life that people she met found intriguing, even though she did nothing to foster it. It appeared that London Society would be no different.

That was fortunate. The more balls and routs she attended, the greater her chances of ferreting out the identity of this scoundrel.

One invitation in particular captured her attention. "Look, Esperanza," she called, as her companion came back down the stairs, *sans* child. "I have been asked to the Duchess of Dacey's ball tonight. The *Gazette* said it is *the* event that opens the Season. It is always a mad crush."

"A crush?" Esperanza sounded doubtful as to the charms of such a thing.

"Yes." Carmen laughed. "Perfect."

* * *

"I have heard that she is a *gypsy*."

"A gypsy? Oh, my dear Millicent, no. I was speaking with Lady Treadwell, who was introduced to her in Paris earlier this year. She said that she is an heiress to a great Spanish family. Perhaps even the *royal* family."

"No, no! I heard that she is a Russian princess, fleeing an unhappy love affair."

Peter leaned against the silk-papered wall of the Duchess of Dacey's grand ballroom, attempting to ignore the cluckings of three matrons who were gathered in front of him, blocking his view of the dancers.

The duchess's ball had become quite a crush, as predicted. Excellent for her reputation as a hostess, but a blighted nuisance if one actually wished to move about. Peter was quite trapped between the three women, a potted palm, and a young couple engaged in a deep flirtation involving a great deal of simpering and giggling.

How they could even converse, let alone flirt, above the confounded racket Peter could not say. The ball was a roaring bore, and Lady Deidra had not even attended. Peter drained his glass of champagne, and glanced again at his watch.

It was all of seven minutes since he had last looked.

He sighed as he tucked the watch away. He loathed London during the Season. Every proud mama had their snares out for him, parading their white muslin-clad darlings before him as if they were at a sale at Tattersall's. The newspapers all referred to him coyly as "that elusive bachelor, the Earl of C," and speculated on which young lady he would eventually settle on. It was quite revolting, and one of the central reasons he was thinking of ending it all by wedding Lady Deidra.

He would never have agreed to come to this, one

of the grandest balls of the Season, if Elizabeth had not begged for his escort.

"It would be so very good for my business, Peter," she had said when he tried to demur. "I absolutely must renew my acquaintance with the duchess, she knows utterly *everyone* in the *ton*."

"Where is your husband? Why can he not take you?" Peter had protested, even as he sensed the futility of it. "Didn't he take some sort of vow at your wedding? For better, for worse, for every rout where there could be potential patrons of the arts?"

"He has gone to inspect that country manor we have just purchased, as I wrote you! Evanstone Park, only a short distance from Clifton!"

So here Peter was, in the corner of a crowded ballroom, drinking poor-quality champagne and listening to some silly women prattle on about some gypsy.

He glanced at his watch again. Almost ten o'clock. Surely he could respectably take his leave now. He forced his way out of the corner, past the matrons, and went in search of his sister.

"Look!" one of the matrons hissed. "It is the Ice Earl! I did not know *he* was in Town. Dangling after the Clearbridge chit, do you think? I did hear . . ."

Peter ignored that silly sobriquet of Ice Earl and the reference to Lady Deidra, and hurried onward, intent on his errand.

Elizabeth was found holding court in a small sitting room off of the ballroom, surrounded by her friends. The diamond bracelets fastened over her kid gloves flashed as she waved her feather fan to emphasize some point.

"Peter!" she called. "Do come and join us. I just heard the most remarkable *on-dit*."

"Oh?" He sat down beside her on her settee, and took another glass of champagne from a nearby tray.

"What is it? That that woman over there in the rather egregious orange satin is a princess of France in disguise?"

Elizabeth wrinkled her nose. "Lud, no! That is quite a horrid frock. What I heard is ever so much better. I heard that the Condesa de Santiago is invited to this ball, and that she has accepted! I did not even know she was in England."

"Who?"

"The Condesa de Santiago. My, but you *have* buried yourself in the country, Peter. Simply everyone has heard of her. I even saw her once at a ball in Venice last year."

"Ah. So we have established that she is famous," Peter answered. "What is she famous for doing?"

One of Elizabeth's friends, a young lady in pink silk, interjected helpfully, "I have heard she is a gypsy."

"No, one of those red Indians from America," said a gentleman in a shocking purple waistcoat.

Elizabeth waved all this away with a flick of her fan. "She is almost Spanish royalty, and she makes her way from one European court to another. She is very beautiful, and very mysterious. To have her at one's ball guarantees it will be a great social success." She glanced scornfully at the man who had expressed the Indian theory. "So I daresay the fact that she is Spanish means she cannot be American, Gerald."

"And Santiago hardly sounds Russian," Peter murmured wryly.

"Her whole name is very long and far too complicated. But what is that about Russia, dear?" said Elizabeth.

"Merely another opinion I heard offered when I was trapped beside a potted palm."

"Really?" Elizabeth's brow arched curiously. "What did you hear?"

"Nothing at all of interest, I fear."

"Pooh! I did want some new tidbit to send on in my next letter to Georgina. We are both quite fascinated with the condesa. Georgina wanted to paint her portrait, but the condesa left Venice before we could meet her."

"Oh, well," said Peter. "If *Georgina Beaumont* is interested . . ."

"Oh, hush! I don't know why you hate Georgina so, she is my dearest friend in the world."

"I think the fact that when last we met she chased me with a fireplace poker had something to do with it."

"That was only because . . ."

A woman wearing an astonishing headdress of flowers and fruit interrupted this familiar brother-sister squabble. "I heard that the condesa was the mistress of a duke."

Elizabeth was appropriately distracted. "Which duke?"

"I did not hear that part," the headdress woman said. "Perhaps it was a marquis."

"But what of the rumor that she was seen in Vienna with Lord Riverton?" said the girl in pink silk.

In spite of himself, Peter was beginning to be intrigued with this condesa. The usual gossip at *ton* affairs was usually completely uninteresting to him, perhaps because he was so often the center of it.

But this seemed rather different from the usual elopements of heiresses with dancing masters and who was seen going into whose room at which country house party.

A condesa, a foreigner whose connections were really quite unknown, who was seen at the finest houses in Europe. A woman of mystery . . .

He had not encountered such an intriguing female in . . . well, in many years.

His jaw tightened at the memory of another dark, mysterious Spanish lady. *Her* name had even been similar to this woman's.

"And she is coming here?" he said, carefully indifferent.

Elizabeth blinked at him in astonishment. "Why, Peter. Never say *you* are interested in the doings of this condesa?"

"This fete has been—less than stimulating. A beautiful lady, whether she be Spanish, Russian, or red Indian, would surely enliven things."

"Even if she does appear, I doubt she would be as lively as all that. One could hope, of course, that she might start clicking castanets in the midst of some staid country-dance." Elizabeth tapped her fan thoughtfully against her chin. "I cannot account for it, brother. Usually you just sigh and roll your eyes at our frivolity."

"I never roll my eyes."

"I beg to differ! So—your curiosity is piqued by the condesa?"

"Perhaps a mere soupçon of pique," Peter grudgingly admitted.

"But what of . . ." Elizabeth's voice fell to a whisper. "What of Yvette Montcalm?"

"I am not going to ask how you came to know that name, Elizabeth."

"You needn't try to freeze me with that tone, Peter. People tell things to artists, you know, while they are forced to sit still for a sitting. Delicious gossip—such as your cozy little *pied-à-terre* on Half Moon Street."

"The mere fact that I listened to your tales of some Spanish woman has nothing at all to do with Madame Montcalm." And he would not yet give his sister the satisfaction of knowing he and Yvette had parted ways.

"Of course not." Elizabeth covered his hand with

her own small one. "I am just glad that all this talk of Spain has not brought on unpleasant thoughts for you."

"You needn't fret, Lizzie. I have put all that nonsense quite behind me."

"Excellent! Then, you must let me introduce you to my new friend Lady Halsby. Nick and I met her in Venice, she is quite lovely . . ."

Peter laughed. "No, Lizzie! I have put Spain quite behind me, true, but that does not signify that I am ready for more of your matchmaking efforts. I will come to parson's mousetrap in my own time, thank you."

"Well, if you do change your mind . . ."

Elizabeth's words were lost as a furor arose among the crowd nearer the ballroom doors. Elizabeth stood and tried to peer above the heads of those around her, stretching on the toes of her satin slippers.

"How very vexing!" she cried. "I cannot see at all."

"It is she!" someone said. "The condesa has arrived."

"Look!"

A sudden hush fell as the doors to the ballroom opened, and the liveried footman announced, in ringing tones and an egregious Spanish accent, "The Condesa Carmen Pilar Maria de Santiago y Montero."

Peter, who was considerably taller than his diminutive sister, had an excellent view over the crowd as a figure appeared in the doorway.

She was tall, taller than most women, with a proud, straight carriage and a horsewoman's slim suppleness. She wore a dashing gown of black and gold lace over deep green satin. Antique gold Etruscan bracelets gleamed over long black gloves.

Her head was turned away as she greeted the

Duchess of Dacey, but beneath the pattern of her black lace mantilla could be seen fashionably cropped night dark curls, interspersed with gold ornaments shaped like tiny jeweled butterflies.

Framed by the inlaid doors, she made quite a dramatic and eye-catching picture. Peter silently applauded the condesa's keen sense of theatricality. It was obvious why she had the entire jaded *ton* eating from her silk-gloved palm.

Then she turned to reveal her face, pale as milk, with huge dark eyes that cooly surveyed the crowd laid out before her.

Peter's champagne glass fell from his fingers to crash onto the marble floor, causing the ladies around him to leap back with startled cries, their skirts clutched against them.

The woman who had just made such a striking entrance was not a gypsy, or a Russian.

She was his wife.

Chapter Three

"Ah, Condesa!" The Duchess of Dacey was almost giggling, the orange plumes in her headdress acquiver, as she took her new guest's arm and drew her into the crowded ballroom. "Such an honor you do my humble soiree!"

Carmen inclined her head in what she hoped was a regal manner, striving to keep her features smooth and mysterious, despite her exhaustion and nervousness. "I do apologize for my late arrival, Your Grace," she murmured.

"Not at all! Why, we have not even gone in to supper yet." The duchess linked her arm through Carmen's and smiled brightly. "But you have not met everyone, Condesa! You are surely acquainted with the Marquis of Stonehurst? He tells me you met in Paris."

"Yes certainly. How do you do?" Carmen held out her gloved hand to the portly little marquis and suffered him to drool over it, wondering if perhaps he could be her letter writer. She had met his brother in Spain, who had then conveniently died and left this man the title. But, no—he was so obviously concerned with only his own comforts. He would not have been concerned with his brother's life in Spain; he would never have heard of Shadow or Alvaro.

Yet, as he attempted to peer down her bodice, she

almost wished it was him. It would have been such a pleasure to skewer the little lecher with her dagger.

"Delighted to see you again, Condesa. It was such a pleasure to dance with you at Madame de Troyes's ball last winter." He smiled up at her in a particularly unpleasant manner. "I hope I may have the honor of dancing with you tonight?"

I would rather sink through the floor and die, Carmen thought. Then she smiled sweetly. "I am sorry, but I do not mean to dance tonight. Now, if you will excuse me . . ." With a small nod, she moved away from the odious marquis and their giggling hostess, and made her own progress across the room.

She paused to speak with those people she had met on her travels, and to be introduced to their friends, who were all eager to make her acquaintance. She smiled, and nodded, and exchanged pleasantries, accepted invitations to take tea and to drive in the park.

Though, behind all this exquisite politeness, she was always watching. Wondering if one of these smooth-faced people, who were drinking champagne and attempting to make witticisms with her, could be the one who had either seen her themselves in Spain, or had a son or brother or husband who did. Wondering which of them thought they held so much of her past, and her future, in their grip.

Where could she even begin? It seemed hopeless.

And this ball did not seem the right atmosphere for making inquiries concerning military service. It was an evening of preliminary reconnaissance only.

At last she managed to evade the crowds and find a quiet corner, a tiny nook curtained in by one of the open French doors leading to the terrace and the gardens. Carmen slipped gratefully behind the heavy velvet draperies and let them fall behind her, enclosing her in silence.

The night air was blessedly cool on her face after the overheated, over-perfumed ballroom. She pushed her mantilla back from her flushed cheeks, and leaned her forehead against the door frame, closing her eyes.

She was utterly exhausted. A ball, particularly one of this magnitude, was the very last place she wanted to be after a long journey. All those silly people, eating and drinking far too much, whispering wicked things about one another—it was all so familiar. London was just Paris, Venice, and Vienna with a different accent.

She shuddered.

If she could follow her own wishes, she would be tucked away beside her own fire, with a new book and nice sherry. And she would assuredly be wearing her favorite old dressing gown, the red velvet with the mended elbow, and not this itchy thing from Madame La Tour's Parisian couturier shop! It was said that the condesa (a creature Carmen considered rather separate from Carmen) was a woman of dashing style, but really fashion was a confounded nuisance.

She tugged the close-fitting lace and satin bodice away from her skin and let some of the cool air onto her shoulders. Yes, she would definitely change into her dressing gown as soon as she arrived home.

But for now she had work to do. What she sought would never be found if she stayed at home by her own fire.

"It will not be for long," she whispered. "It will all soon be over."

Carmen straightened her shoulders, and smoothed her bodice in preparation to rejoin the ball.

"Ah, the Condesa de Santiago, I presume. I have heard much about you," a low, velvet soft voice murmured behind her.

Someone had joined her, undetected, in her safe nest. Another who fancied himself an "admirer," no doubt. Carmen pasted on a bright smile and turned.

A gasp escaped her lips before she could catch it. "Peter! *Madre de Dios*, is it you? But it cannot be!"

"My sentiments precisely," he answered, his blue gaze flickering over her in freezing examination. "Carmen."

The room spun about her head; there was such a roaring in her ears, like a dozen rushing rivers. She fell back against the door, hardly able to remain standing. She covered her face with her gloved hands.

"You are not going to swoon, are you?" he said. His voice was exactly the same, just as she heard it so often in her haunted dreams. Like warm brandy.

"No," she replied. And promptly collapsed at his feet.

"By Jove, Carmen! Never say you have become a frail flower of a female." He scooped her up easily in his arms, and nudged open the door with his shoulder.

She felt the cool air on her shoulders and face as he pushed back the lace of her mantilla. "Certainly not," she managed to gasp, still overcome by the hazy sense of unreality. "I am far too tall to ever earn the sobriquet of 'frail flower.' It is only you English and your overheated rooms. I could not even catch my breath." She looked up at him, wondering if everyone talked of such things as the temperature when faced with long-dead husbands.

She rather thought not.

"My apologies," Peter said, "on behalf of all the English who overheat their rooms."

He placed her carefully on her feet, and she leaned against the marble balustrade of the terrace, grateful for its cold solidity.

She studied him in the moonlight, this stranger she had once known so very well. He was as beautiful as ever, an Apollo with hair as bright as winter sunlight, tall and elegantly slim. But there was something there that had not been six years ago. Deep lines bracketed his lovely mouth; his eyes were as flat and still as a millpond, no stirring of emotion at seeing her again. It was almost as if another soul had come to inhabit the body of the man she loved.

How could *her* Peter be behind those eyes?

"I thought you dead," she managed to say. "They told me you were killed that day."

"Ah, my dear. What an impasse. I thought *you* were dead."

"Me? Dead? Whoever told you that?"

He shrugged, the deep blue velvet of his coat rippling impressively over the smooth muscles of his shoulders. At least he had not become soft over the years. He was still sleek and strong as a tiger.

"I do not recall," he answered. "But now I see that you are very much alive." His eyes slid over her dazzling décolletage. "And unscarred. Come to finish the job, darling?"

Carmen started. "Job?" Surely he could not know of *that*. They had not seen each other in so long; he could not know of the letters, of why she had come to England. Despite his sorcerer's eyes, he could not read her mind.

Could he?

She suddenly became very interested in the fan she held in her hands. She opened and closed the gold-and-black lace. "Whatever do you mean? I am here only to enjoy your London Season."

Peter's patrician features were tight, his hands curled at his sides. "I am talking of your job of betraying my regiment six years ago."

If he had suddenly reached out and struck her

across the face, Carmen could not have been more shocked. It seemed one shock too many. Her fan fell from her fingers, its delicate sticks shattering on the marble at their feet.

Major Chauvin had said those many years ago that she would be blamed for the demise of the Fifteenth Light Dragoons, and thus might as well tell him all she knew anyway. Somehow she had not believed him. Had not believed that Peter could ever think such a thing of her.

"Betrayed?" she whispered.

"Yes. You do remember the day after our wedding? Nicholas Hollingsworth almost died that day. Many men did die."

"Nicholas!" Carmen remembered the dark, laughing man, who, next to Peter, had been the most handsome man of the regiment. A wave of nausea broke over her. She turned away from Peter, her hand pressed to her mouth. "No. I would not do such a thing."

Peter took her arm and turned her to face him. His grasp was hard. "I saw you, Carmen! Riding away from the battle with Chauvin, cradled in his arms." He shook her. "You knew of our troop movements. Did you run to him immediately after our wedding, from my bed to his? Did you, Carmen? Is that why you were so insistent on riding off by yourself?"

Six years of anger and grief shone in his eyes as he pulled her against him, drawing her up on tiptoe, her breasts pressed against his chest.

"Have you come to kill me?" he whispered.

"'Tis you who are killing me, Peter!" Tears coursed unchecked over her cheeks and chin, spotting her expensive bodice. This man could not be her husband! Peter had been hard at times, yes, but never cruel. She pushed futilely against his chest, unable to bear his warm nearness, his familiar scent. "I never did those things you say."

"Then, prove it! Prove you never betrayed me. Betrayed the love we had between us. I have been in torment for so long."

"How can I prove anything? It was so long ago, a lifetime," she sobbed. "You are obviously set against me in your heart, and have been for a long time. Nothing I say now could change that, could it? I claim innocence on my mother's soul. That is all I can do."

"Carmen!" He shook her arm again, and her ivory comb and lace mantilla slipped free from their fastenings and tangled at their feet.

Desperate to be free, Carmen lashed out, slapping him once across the face. He immediately released her, and fell back, trembling.

A thin line of blood had appeared at his lip. He touched it lightly, and Carmen stared down at her left hand as if it did not belong to her at all. Slowly she peeled off the black silk glove, and they both looked down at the ring that had caught his lip. A large square-cut emerald.

She folded her fingers into a fist.

"Carmen," Peter whispered. "I did not . . ." He was as pale as the marble of the terrace as he stared at that ring.

"Peter! There you are at last. I had quite despaired of finding you. It is time for supper, and I am famished. You did say that . . ."

The tiny woman in blue silk, who had glided out onto the terrace behind them, stopped abruptly when she saw that Peter was not alone.

"Oh," she said. "I do beg your pardon."

Carmen bent to retrieve her mantilla, and arranged it carefully over her hair, bringing the lacy folds forward to conceal her tearstained face. "No, no, I beg *your* pardon, *Señorita*. I was just leaving."

"Condesa de Santiago!" the woman cried. She rushed forward to seize Carmen's bare left hand in her own small, gloved ones. "This is such an honor! I have been quite longing to meet you. Have you yet had your portrait painted in England?"

"My portrait?" Carmen glanced in bewilderment over the woman's dark head to Peter, who was still as stone.

"Yes! Oh. I must seem very rag-mannered to you. Since my brother appears to have been struck quite mute, I shall introduce myself. I am Lady Elizabeth Hollingsworth, nee Everdean."

"Brother?" Carmen looked down at the tiny, black-haired elf, who looked not a bit like the tall, golden Peter.

"Stepbrother, actually. I am an artist, and I should so love to paint your portrait." Elizabeth dug about in her pearl-beaded reticule. "Here is my card. Do send me word when you are settled. You must come to Clifton House, to take tea with me."

Carmen blinked down at the small square of pale blue vellum. "Hollingsworth? Such as Nicholas?"

Elizabeth's eyes widened. "Yes! He is my husband. Do you know him?"

"Only—only by reputation," Carmen murmured.

Elizabeth laughed merrily. "Oh-ho, yes! So very many people do."

Carmen smiled slightly and backed away toward the steps that led to the garden. "Do excuse me, Lady Elizabeth, but I really must depart. It grows very late."

"Certainly! But, please, do call on me. Or allow me to call on you."

"Yes, of course. Good night." Carmen picked up her skirts and fled into the darkness of the garden, unmindful of the mud that sucked at her thin slippers. She only wanted to be away from there, so she could think quietly.

Elizabeth watched her flight with a frown, then turned back to her pale brother. "Peter? Whatever did you say to the poor woman?"

Peter shook his head and gave her an odd little half smile. "Why, nothing, Lizzie. I merely complimented her on her—sense of fashion."

"Fashion? Do you mean you complimented her gown?"

"Yes, something of that sort. Shall we go in to supper?"

"Certainly. I hear that the duchess's lobster patties are quite divine."

Yet even as Peter took Elizabeth's arm to escort her back into the ballroom, he could not resist looking back to where Carmen had disappeared into the night.

Then he saw, gleaming against the marble, the carved ivory comb that had fallen from the folds of Carmen's mantilla. He picked it up and secreted it inside his coat.

Surely its owner would miss it.

Chapter Four

Home at last.

Carmen locked the front door behind her and made her weary way up the shadowed stairs to her bedchamber. Esperanza had seen to the airing of the room, and the bedclothes were turned back to reveal fresh linens. A fire burned merrily in the grate, and set on a small table before it was a light repast of tea sandwiches, a pot of tea, and a bottle of her favorite sherry.

Her stomach rumbled, reminding her of the mundanities of life, such as the fact that she had missed supper, and the duchess's fabled lobster patties.

Madame La Tour's stylish gown was rather difficult to remove alone, but Carmen managed to wriggle out of it, and left it and the mantilla in a heap on the floor. She turned toward her full-length mirror, and almost thought a stranger was staring back at her.

She looked like a wraith, silvery-white in the firelight, her eyes huge and her dark, short hair tangled over her ears. Even her nudity, the tall, angular body she had despaired of all her life, seemed not her own. She looked, and felt, quite otherworldly.

Everything had turned top-over-tail, the whole existence she had painfully built for herself, and it seemed certain that it could never go right side up again.

Peter was alive! She had hoped, oh, a thousand times that she could she him again, just once, to touch his face, feel his arms about her. For just a glimpse of his smile, she would have given her own soul.

Now it seemed her prayers were answered. He was *alive*! Yet how he had changed. He seemed so old now, as old as she herself often felt, and so very hard. And his anger toward her was a very powerful force; it had obviously been festering inside him for six years, poisoning all they had once had, and hoped to have, together.

Carmen's hand drifted over her pale midriff, to her belly above the white silk drawers, across the faint stretch marks from when she had been carrying Isabella inside of her. She had been a small baby, but so active, always kicking and turning . . .

Isabella!

Carmen pressed her fist to her mouth to muffle a sudden cry. What if Peter came to hear of Isabella? What if he saw her, this golden-blond child? He would doubtless guess the truth in an instant.

And she, though titled, was a foreigner. She would be powerless against the Earl of Clifton if he decided to take their child.

"That cannot happen," she said aloud, fiercely.

A knock sounded at the door, startling her. She grabbed up her dressing gown and slipped it over her nakedness. "Yes?"

Esperanza peered around the door, her wrinkled face framed by an absurd pink ruffled nightcap. "Carmencita! You are home early."

Carmen forced herself to smile lightly. "It is hardly early, after one."

"That is early for you. You are usually gone until the dawn." Was there a hint of disapproval in her tired voice? If there was, it was concealed as she bustled about the room, shaking out the discarded gown and locating hastily kicked off slippers. "Did you have a good time at the ball?"

"Hm, not really. It was such a dreadful crush, just as everyone said it would be. I could not breathe at all. And so many things happened . . ."

"Things such as what, Carmencita?"

Carmen shook her head. "I will tell all later, Esperanza, but I am too tired now." She sat down beside the fire and poured herself a liberal amount of the sherry. "I cannot remember when I was last so tired."

Esperanza eyed the sherry. "You should eat something before you drink that, Carmencita. Did you have supper at the ball?"

"No, more is the pity! I heard that the duchess's lobster patties are delightful."

"Then, you must eat those sandwiches. You look pale as the grave."

Carmen gave an unladylike snort. "Thank you, Esperanza, for that encouraging compliment!" But she did pop a cucumber sandwich into her mouth.

Esperanza nodded in satisfaction, and bent to pick up the mantilla. "Carmen!"

"Yes?"

"Did you not wear your ivory comb tonight?"

Carmen's hand flew to her hair. "Oh, no! It must have fallen at the ball."

"How could that have happened? We used ever so many pins!"

Carmen closed her eyes and shook her head. "It simply fell, that is all. I will send a note 'round to the duchess tomorrow, and see if anyone found it in her ballroom."

"That comb belonged to your mama," Esperanza

clucked. "Really, Carmen, sometimes you are so very careless."

Esperanza was always quick to point out her short-comings, and had done so ever since Carmen's baby-hood. "I am certain someone will have discovered it. But I am far too tired to think of it now!"

"My poor *niña*," Esperanza cooed, her irritation forgotten. "You must sleep. I know something did happen tonight, something terrible you are not telling me. I can see it in your eyes. But I will wait."

Carmen kissed Esperanza's cheek. "I *will* tell you later. Now, dear one, good night."

"Buenos noches, niña."

When Esperanza had gone, Carmen climbed grate-fully between her cool sheets and fell into deep, dream-plagued sleep.

At last Peter was alone in his bedchamber. It was nearly dawn; a few gray-pink tendrils were reaching through the curtains. Yet it had still taken several protestations of complete exhaustion on his part to persuade his chattering sister to cease prattling about the ball and retire to her chamber.

He splashed cold water from a basin onto his face, unmindful of the damp spots that appeared on his open shirt and scattered across his chest. When he lifted his eyes to the small shaving mirror, the face that stared back at him was positively haggard. Haggard, and pale, and . . . haunted.

Could Elizabeth have been right when she expressed concern for him in the carriage on their way home? Was his old madness coming back upon him?

Peter pushed away from the mirror with a muttered curse. It could not be. He had fought too hard to overcome his ghosts, to come back to the light and try to make a life for himself where he could not hurt anyone ever again. He would not give in to that darkness again, even if he *had* held a ghost in his arms that night.

The darkness, what Elizabeth called his spells, had come over him when he had returned from Spain, wounded in both body and spirit. *Home* was not as he had remembered it, not the fantasy he had longed for when he had lain alone in a Spanish field hospital. Elizabeth had grown up into a dark beauty in his absence, with an iron will of her own that he had not been prepared to deal with. And her every glance at him had spoken of how frightened she was of the monster he had become. It finally forced her to run away.

Six years ago, on that fateful day, he had thought Nicholas Hollingsworth, his best friend, dead. Yet fortunately he had lived and was now married to his sister. However, Peter had thought Carmen not only dead, but had later learned she was their betrayer.

Now he saw that Carmen was not dead, and the realization was vexing. She was here, in England, healthy and whole, and more beautiful than she had ever been even in his dreams.

Why had she come into his life again, opening old wounds and reminding him of the foolish dreams he had once cherished? Peter could not flatter himself that she had come to England to find *him*. She had been so obviously shocked to see him; as shocked as he was to see her.

To see that emerald on her finger.

Carmen, dead Carmen, was the famous condesa. It was strange, a nightmare—a dream. But he also could not ignore the deep joy that had coursed through him when he had first glimpsed her face.

Then his eye caught on the ivory comb he had tossed onto the bed, gleaming against the burgundy velvet counterpane. He reached for it, turning it over and over on his palm.

Its cool smoothness against his skin, callused from riding, reminded him that this was a nightmare, or a dream, that had become all too real.

Chapter Five

"Look, Peter, here is an account of the ball last night!" In her excitement Elizabeth rattled the newspaper so vehemently that her morning chocolate sloshed out of her cup onto the white damask tablecloth.

"Indeed?" Peter did not look up from his letters, which he had not actually read a word of since he had sat down.

"Indeed! And we are mentioned."

"*You* are always mentioned, Lizzie. You cannot step from the front door without causing a stir these days."

"Hm, but here they have actually gone to the trouble of describing my gown and jewels. Usually they just say I was there. See here, 'cerulean silk trimmed in white alençon lace and satin rosebuds, created by the new couturier Madame Auverge, and the stunning Everdean pearls.' My consequence must be increasing. This is excellent, since I am unveiling Lady Kingsley's portrait at a small soiree next week, and I think it is quite the finest work I have done thus far. The portrait, and my being mentioned at all the right gatherings, should mean even more commissions." She scanned the rest of the column. "Do you not want to know what they say about you?"

"What do they say? That I wore a 'stunning'

blue—no, cerulean—coat, created by Weston?"
Peter smirked.

"No, much better by far! They report that you appeared quite fascinated by the lovely Condesa de Santiago, who is recently arrived from the Continent, and that you were seen escorting her onto the terrace."

Peter's coffee cup slipped from his hand, but he did not even notice the hot stain that spread across his new doeskin breeches. He frowned at his grinning sister, who he wouldn't put it past to have sent that little tidbit in to the papers herself. "Scandalous rag! What is it you are reading, Elizabeth? They shall be out of print by the end of the day."

"Why?" Elizabeth's eyes widened innocently. "Is it not true? Were you not on the terrace with the condesa? Locked in an embrace?"

"It was not like that." Peter's jaw was taut.

"Not like—what? She is beautiful, is she not? And rather familiar-seeming, as well."

"What are you talking about?"

"The condesa, of course. Quite intriguing. I was beginning to have hopes that your tastes are improving. That actress Yvette . . ." Elizabeth frowned. "I have never seen that shade of blonde in nature."

"Yvette is hardly a suitable topic for a man to discuss with his sister, Elizabeth. Besides which . . ."

"Oh, how every vexing! I did so want to 'discuss it,' " Elizabeth cried.

"Also, if you would please not interrupt, I have some other news for you."

"Really?" Elizabeth blithely reached for the butter. "What is that?"

"I have decided to make an offer for Lady Deidra Clearbridge."

Elizabeth's reaction was not at all what he had expected. The piece of toast she was buttering fell from her hand and landed butter-side-down on the lap of her green morning gown. Her jaw gaped. "You are what?"

"Going to offer for Lady Deidra Clearbridge. I thought that would make you happy. You are always harping at me to make a respectable match and set up my nursery. I am going to do so." As soon as he could figure out what to do with the very-much-alive first Countess of Clifton.

"First of all, I do not *harp*! And Lady Deidra is not at all what I could have wished for. She is such a milk-and-water miss." Elizabeth's nose wrinkled.

"Living in Italy has made you bold, Lizzie. Lady Deidra is perfectly proper."

"You would run her over in a month, Peter! I know you. The condesa is much more your style."

Peter tossed down his letters and rose to his feet. "I must go out, if you will excuse me, Lizzie."

"You are avoiding the subject, as usual. Where are you going? And are you going like that?" She looked pointedly at the large coffee stain on his leg.

"I was going to go upstairs and change, but if you think I could start a new fashion . . ."

"You *are* in a mood this morning. But if you do not want to tell me where you are going, I certainly have no wish to know."

Peter laughed and bent down to kiss her cheek. "I am in a 'mood' because of the late night last night, thanks to my social sister! I am an old man, and need my sleep."

"You? Old? Ha! I have more gray in my hair than you."

"You, dear, are eternally young. And when is your husband coming to Town, O Goddess of Youth?"

"The day after tomorrow, thankfully! I need his assistance in planning a house party at our new country manor, since I know that *you* will be of no help."

"Well, do try to stay out of trouble until then." He started to turn away.

Elizabeth caught his hand, suddenly serious. "Peter, dear, are you quite certain you have been well? You look rather pale this morning, and I think that . . . well, I know you said you have not had any spells of late, and I believe you, but . . ."

"Lizzie," Peter interrupted. "I am really quite well. And now I must be going. I have an appointment that I must keep." He kissed her cheek again, and left the breakfast room.

Elizabeth watched him go, worrying with her teeth at her lower lip. "Don't forget!" she called. "We are engaged to attend Lady Castleton's musicale tonight."

Across Town, another pair of eyes scanned the same newspaper over the breakfast table.

"Scandalous!" Carmen hissed. "Deep in enraptured conversation, indeed. I think this paper must employ the same writers that create your horrid novels, Esperanza."

"Mama?" a little voice piped up. "What are you reading? Can I see it?"

"*May* I see it, and no you may not. You do not know how to read yet, anyway, *niña*, and when you can you will read more edifying literature than this rag." Carmen made a concerted effort to smooth the frown from her face. She folded the paper, placed it carefully beside her plate, and smiled at her daughter.

"I can so read! A bit. Esperanza is teaching me to write my name." While her mother's attention had been turned, Isabella had systematically demolished her toast into minuscule crumbs. She carefully picked up one of the crumbs with one sticky fingertip and popped it into her mouth. "But it is a very long name, Mama. Why could you not have named me Mary? It's much shorter."

"Isabella was your *abuela*'s name!" said Esperanza, crossing herself as she always did at the mention of Carmen's long-dead, sainted mother. "You should honor it, Isabella." Then she swept out of the room to fetch the morning post, black bombazine skirts rustling.

Carmen watched her leave, puzzled at her cross behavior. "Indeed, it is your grandmother's name, Bella, and a pretty name, too." She reached out with her napkin to wipe Isabella's small chin. "And soon, we shall find you a governess, to teach you to behave like the fine lady your grandmother was."

Isabella pulled a face. "I do not need a governess! I have you and Esperanza."

Carmen tousled Isabella's already tumbled golden curls. When she made that stubborn, set-jawed face, the child looked so like her father. "Certainly you need a governess. She will be able to teach you so much more than we can."

"But, Mama . . ."

Carmen held one finger to her lips. "No more, Bella. But if you are very good this morning, perhaps we could go to Gunter's for ices this afternoon."

Isabella brightened. "Really?"

"Really. But only if you have a bath and let Esperanza dress you in your new pink frock."

Esperanza came back into the breakfast room at that moment, the letters on a silver tray. She smiled, her earlier dark mood apparently forgotten. "So very many invitations again, Carmencita!"

"Thank you, Esperanza. It would appear so." Carmen surveyed the thick stack of cards and letters. Thankfully, there were no missives sealed with black wax today. "My, but we are becoming popular! Here is an invitation to a supper party at the home of the Marchioness of Penshurst, an invitation to the opera . . . but what is this?" She held up a letter written on rich, pale blue stationery, neatly folded and sealed with an elaborate *E* pressed into darker blue wax. She tore it open and read aloud, "My dear Condesa, please forgive me for writing to you so quickly after our meeting. I know we were not properly introduced at the Duchess of Dacey's ball, but we are women of the world, and can overlook such silliness! If you are not otherwise engaged, could you take tea with me this afternoon? I am quite longing to become better acquainted with you. Sincerely, Lady Elizabeth Hollingsworth."

"Hollingsworth?" Esperanza said. "The lady artist we heard of when we were in Italy?"

"The very one. I met her at the ball last night. She said she would like to paint my portrait; she was very charming. And she was married to one of the English officers I knew during the war." Carmen did not mention the fact that Elizabeth was, in reality, her own sister-in-law. She had told Esperanza, long ago when she had arrived home enceinte, that she had been married briefly. But she had never said to whom, and she had always thought Esperanza only half believed that she had been legally wed. It seemed rather ill timed to bring it up now.

"Carmen, this is wonderful!" Esperanza cried. "This Lady Elizabeth is so well-known."

"Hm, yes, she is. But I really don't have time to sit for another portrait now." She carefully folded the letter. "You are right, though, Esperanza dear, in saying that she is quite well-known. Patrons are lined up to have her paint their portrait, and she does me great honor in requesting I sit for her. So I shall have tea with her. After I look at these letters of application for the post of governess."

After quieting Isabella's protests about the governess, Carmen sent her off with Esperanza to be washed and dressed for the day. Then she retreated to the small room that would be her library, a cozy room with deep, comfortable sofas and chairs, and crates of well-loved books waiting to be unpacked and placed on the empty shelves. From the tall windows, she could see the small park across the way, where children and nursemaids were gathering.

She had hopes that soon this room would feel a haven of quiet from the world.

Today, it was not.

She sat down at her little French desk to pen a reply to Elizabeth's letter, but somehow the polite, simple words would not come. Instead, she sat, chin in hand, and watched that park, watched the children at play.

Was she making a mistake in responding, even in a small way, to Elizabeth's friendly overtures? She genuinely liked her, even on such brief acquaintance. She was merry and charming, unafraid to go after what she wanted; Carmen sensed that they could well be kindred, unconventional spirits. And Carmen remembered well Elizabeth's handsome, funny husband.

But Elizabeth was also Peter's sister.

Peter, who had become so bitter that he no longer seemed the same gallant man she had once known, once loved. The years had changed him so.

Just as they had changed her.

Carmen twisted the emerald on her finger, finding its familiar weight comforting. No, she was not the same idealistic girl she had been then. Despite the disappointments of her first marriage, the horrors of war, she had been so full of romantic hopes and dreams.

Peter had seemed almost a fairy tale then, a knight who would carry her away from the fears and the danger with only his kiss. But, of course, that had been an illusion. He had died and left her alone, and she had carried on as best she could. It had not been a fairy tale by any means, her life of travel and searching, but she had survived. She had even carved out a measure of happiness with her little girl.

If Peter discovered Isabella, he could take her away if he chose. He had seemed quite angry enough last night to so choose. That would be the one thing that could shatter Carmen's life utterly and beyond repair.

Perhaps it would be better if she left England right away, and be damned to the blackmailer. She could go to Russia, or America, or anywhere far away where no one could find her daughter.

And yet . . . she could not ignore the way her heart sang when she saw his face again, his beautiful face. She had longed to throw herself against his chest, to bury her face against his neck and inhale his well-remembered scent, to feel his arms safely around her again.

Those warm Spanish nights they had shared had come rushing back to her in that moment, and it was as if the years had never passed.

She had missed Peter terribly, for six long years. And she had seen the look on his face when he saw the moonlight flash on her ring. He had missed her, too.

Despite the lies and the misunderstandings, he had missed her.

If only the years and experience did not lie between them. And so very many secrets.

Carmen pressed her hands against her eyes, trying

to hold back the flood of futile tears that threatened to flow.

A knock sounded at the closed door.

"Carmen?" Esperanza called. "Are you there?"

Carmen blinked fiercely and scrubbed at her cheeks. She picked up her pen and tried to appear unruffled. "Yes, Esperanza, what is it?"

Esperanza opened the door and came in, her silver tray bearing a single calling card held before her. "You have a visitor. A *man*." Her sniff conveyed her disapproval.

"A man? It is not my at-home day. Whoever can it be?" She reached for the card and stared down at the elegant script printed there:

Peter Everdean, the Earl of Clifton.

She turned it over and read the one word scrawled there in pencil.

Please.

"*Madre de Dios*," she whispered. "What is he doing here? How did he find my house?"

Well. It seemed there was nothing for it. She would just have to see him.

Chapter Six

Carmen smoothed her hair for the fifth time, staring intently into the mirror, but not really seeing the neat fall of short curls bound by a blue satin ribbon. She was only searching for excuses *not* to enter the drawing room.

Peter waited for her there. Peter, here, in her very home.

She was only glad that Esperanza had been able to slip Isabella down the back stairs for her outing, with no questions asked.

She glanced at the small clock on her library mantel, and realized that he had been waiting for almost fifteen minutes. Carmen was many things, but she hoped that *rude* was not one of them! She patted her hair once more, smoothed the skirts of her blue muslin morning gown, and went to meet her fate.

His back was to her as he studied the view out of her windows, but even so he quite overwhelmed the small drawing room. His elegant doeskin breeches, blue coat, and champagne polished boots gleamed among her well-loved, well-traveled, if rather battered Spanish antiques. A mahogany walking stick and a pair of butter-soft chamois gloves rested on a crate of still-to-be-unpacked paintings.

Carmen nudged a doll that lay on the carpet beneath a chair with the toe of her slipper, and gathered her Indian cashmere shawl closer about her shoulders. "Good morning, Peter. Such a surprise to see you."

He turned and smiled at her, an oddly sweet, crooked half smile. One she remembered so well that she almost forgot to breathe.

"Not a very pleasant surprise, eh, Carmen?" he said quietly.

She looked away to conceal her breathlessness and bewilderment, and sat down on the nearest chair, arranging her skirts carefully. "Not at all, I assure you." Then she looked up at him again. He seemed more *her* Peter in the fresh morning light, not so much the intimidating earl as he had been in the modish surroundings of a *ton* ball. Now, when she watched his familiar face, it seemed almost as if they had been apart for only moments, not years.

"Indeed?" His golden brow arched. "I gathered from your rather precipitate departure last night that a visit from the devil himself might be more welcome."

Carmen had to almost sit upon her hands to stop herself from reaching out, from touching him to be certain he was real. "I thought of nothing else last night but our meeting," she confessed.

"Neither did I." He took a step closer to her, so close that she could breathe of his clean, sandalwood soap scent. He reached out his hand, very slowly, to touch her cheek.

Carmen could have wept. She closed her eyes and leaned her head slightly, infinitesimally, into the warmth of his palm.

"Carmen," he whispered, his voice low and agonized. "You are *alive*."

"Yes," she answered softly. "I am now."

"I thought never to see you again. But—how?"

She opened her eyes and smiled up at him. "I might ask you the very same question."

"Ah, Carmen," he sighed. "What a pair we are."

"I looked for you," she said. "At the hospital. The surgeon who was still there told me that you, or rather 'that bloke,' had died."

Peter's mouth tightened. His hand fell away from her cheek. "The hospital. I was not there for long, and in the confusion, I am sure it was easy to assume my demise. I was wounded while carrying Nicholas to the hospital, but not seriously. They sent me to Madrid, then home."

Carmen remembered well the anguish of that long-ago day when she had stumbled, pregnant and ill, into the almost empty hospital, only to be told of his death, the death of most of the regiment. "Fortune has been against us," she murmured.

"Yes, fortune has not been kind to us, has it?"

She looked up at him, at his smile, so warm only moments before, now sardonic and empty. "Why are you here, Peter? You have never been the sort to dwell on the past in a sentimental fashion."

"No, indeed I have not. Though I must say it is a rather tempting prospect in the present circumstances. I am rather curious as to what the famous condesa has been doing since our little interlude in Spain."

Carmen swallowed a bitter retort. She waved her hand airily, her emerald catching the sunlight from the window and reflecting it back to him. "Oh, this and that. Many amusing things. Nothing of consequence."

"Becoming quite the toast of the Continent, so I hear." There was barely controlled, fierce anger in his voice.

"There *was* that. But if you think me so wicked as to betray the entire Fifteenth to their deaths, then why do you care what I have been doing?"

There. It was said at last, and there was no recalling it.

Peter flushed a dull red. "Yet you claim innocence in the whole affair."

Carmen rose to face him, her own cheeks decidedly warm. "I do not *claim* it; it is the truth! I had nothing to do with that ambush at Alvaro. I was a victim of it."

"You needn't flash that Spanish temper at me! I saw you, riding away with Chauvin. I heard that . . ." He bit his words off abruptly.

"If you have based your suspicions on that flimsy piece of evidence, then you never knew me at all," Carmen interrupted.

"No," he said. "I suppose I did not."

Peter stared down at Carmen, at her flushed cheeks, her long, elegant hands curled into fists, as if she longed to plant him a facer. A surging joy threatened to overcome years of anger.

Oh, dear Lord, this was *Carmen*. Carmen, alive and beautiful, within reach of his arms. Not the elegant condesa, but *his* Carmen. The woman whose laughter and kisses had been his only refuge in the darkest days of war. His love, his wife.

She stared at him now with a flash of rage in her dark eyes. She was so furious, so full of righteous anger.

Could she have been innocent of what he had thought for so long? Could his eyes have deceived him?

"And I never knew *you*," she said quietly, interrupting these tumultuous thoughts. "Not truly."

"Once, you knew me better than anyone else ever did," he answered.

"I thought so, too. Once." Carmen twisted her ring on her finger. "Why did you come here today, Peter? To hurl some more accusations?"

"No, indeed. I came to give you this." He reached inside his coat and took out her missing comb, carefully wrapped in a handkerchief.

"Thank you." She took the comb from him, her fingertips brushing ever so briefly against his palm. "I was afraid I had lost it forever."

"Yes," he said softly. "Some things when lost are irredeemable, are they not?"

Carmen looked up at him steadily. "Yes."

He wanted, with all his being, to say something more, but he knew not what. His hand lifted, just the merest amount, toward her. Then it fell back to his side. "Well, I shall inconvenience you no longer, Condesa. I shall say good afternoon."

Carmen smoothed her skirts carefully again, appearing unaffected and slightly bored with the whole scene. But her cheekbones were flushed. "Good afternoon. And thank you."

"Thanks? For what?"

"For returning my comb, of course."

"Ah, yes. Of course." He gave her a small bow and turned to leave.

"Peter?" she called after him.

He looked back to her, one brow arched inquiringly. "Yes?"

"I . . . well. I just wanted to say . . . good day." Carmen could feel herself blushing again, but she could not remember at all what it was she had wanted so desperately to say.

He smiled then, and nodded. "Good day."

Then he was gone, his footfalls fading on the tiled floor of her foyer and the front door clicking shut behind him.

She waited until she saw his phaeton go past her window and out of sight, then she collapsed onto the sofa, her face buried in a velvet cushion.

"You *widgeon*!" she moaned. "How could you have been so cabbage-headed as to actually *speak* to him?"

She could have kicked her heels in utter vexation. She even did, just a bit.

But it did not make her feel one jot better.

"Oh, Condesa! What a very charming house. And so kind of you to have me here for tea."

Lady Elizabeth Hollingsworth settled herself comfortably on a satin settee, spreading her peach muslin skirts about her. Even the feathers in her fashionable hat seemed alive with enthusiasm.

"Not at all," Carmen replied, carefully pouring out tea from her silver Russian samovar. Her hands were trembling so she feared she would spill some, and that would be quite embarrassing! "I was quite looking forward to your visit. I know so few people in London."

"But you seemed to know everyone at the Dacey ball!" Then Elizabeth leaned forward eagerly. "You have considered sitting for a portrait?"

Carmen laughed at Elizabeth's zealousness, the abrupt change of subject. "Perhaps! I understand that your work is wonderfully fine. But not any time soon, I fear. I have only just arrived, as you can see, Lady Elizabeth. My house is still in chaos."

Elizabeth looked about at the boxes, the disarranged furniture, the paintings propped against the walls. "Pooh! This is hardly chaos. You should see my home in Venice. *That* is chaos. And you must call me just Elizabeth. Or Lizzie."

"Very well, if you will call me Carmen." She offered the plate of Esperanza's delectable almond cakes.

"Well, then, Carmen. What exactly is between you and my brother?" Elizabeth popped a cake into her mouth, and watched Carmen expectantly.

Carmen nearly choked on the sip of tea she had just taken. She blotted with her napkin at the amber droplets that had fallen onto the silk bodice of her gown. "I scarcely know your brother, La—Elizabeth."

Elizabeth smiled sympathetically. "Yes, so he says. He thinks I am completely fooled. But I am an artist, you know; a student of human nature, in many ways. And I would be very surprised indeed if you had truly only met last night."

"Elizabeth . . ." Carmen's voice trailed away as Elizabeth turned her wide gray eyes toward her. Somehow she, who had lived with lies for years, could not lie to this woman. "Yes."

"You knew him in Spain, did you not?"

"Yes," Carmen whispered. "Did you know . . . ?"

Elizabeth shrugged. "I saw a miniature of you once. You have changed a bit since it was painted, certainly. You are thinner, and the short hair makes such a difference. But your eyes are the same."

"Then, you know?"

"Yes. Peter told me, the day he showed me the painting. Quite reluctantly, I might add. He probably wanted to keep you a secret eternally. But that was when he thought you dead. Everything is changed now, of course."

Carmen couldn't help but laugh at Elizabeth's tone, so blithe in such a strange situation. "Yes, everything is changed now. Not necessarily for the better."

Elizabeth munched on another cake. "How can you say that? Of course it is for the better! It is like a—a novel, a romantic novel. He thought you dead . . ."

"As I thought him."

"Yes. It was very sad, Carmen; he almost went insane from mourning you! Yet you have found each other again. It will mean the end of—less satisfactory things, and we shall all grow old and fat together, watching our children play."

If only. "Oh, Elizabeth. What a lovely picture. And so lovely of you to accept me so swiftly. But there are so many complications. Too many, I think."

"Nonsense! What possible complication could override the fact that you have found each other again so miraculously . . ."

"Mama, Mama!" A tiny, golden-haired whirlwind chose just that moment to fly into the drawing room and throw her arms about her mother's waist. Her pink hair ribbons were quite undone, the ends trailing from her curls, and her skirt hem was muddied. Yet nothing, not even hoydenism, could disguise the patrician perfection of her small face.

"Esperanza took me to the park!" she said, oblivious to their guest. "We fed the ducks, and saw lots of other children, and ladies all dressed up. Will you walk with me tomorrow, Mama? I was so very, very good, so can we go to Gunter's now, please?"

Carmen put her arms around her daughter and held her very close, despite the mud. She looked at Elizabeth over the tangle of Isabella's bright curls.

Elizabeth's mouth was agape. "Oh," she whispered.

Carmen pressed a kiss atop Isabella's head. "We will go to Gunter's soon, darling, when you have washed and changed your dress. But right now Mama has a guest."

"Oh!" Isabella spun about, then pressed back into her mother's skirts, suddenly shy.

"Introduce yourself, dear," Carmen prompted.

"I am Isabella de Santiago," the child said, bobbing a small curtsy. "How do you do."

Elizabeth smiled. "How do you do, Miss Isabella. I am Lady Elizabeth Hollingsworth, but you must call me Lizzie. Your mother and I are becoming friends, and I am sure that you and I will be, too."

Isabella took a tentative step toward her. "You are very pretty," she announced.

Elizabeth laughed merrily. "So are you, Miss Isabella!"

"Are you coming to Gunter's with us?"

Elizabeth looked up at Carmen. "Well, that is for your mother to say. But I do adore a strawberry ice."

Carmen hesitated only a moment. After all, Elizabeth had already seen Isabella. Had realized the truth. What harm could come of accompanying them for ices?

And Carmen did truly like Peter's sister. *Her* sister now, she supposed.

"Of course," she said. "We would love for you to accompany us."

Chapter Seven

Carmen watched distractedly in the mirror as Esperanza brushed out her short black curls and bound them with a fillet of amethysts and pearls.

"Am I making a mistake?" she murmured to herself.

"A mistake?" Esperanza answered, herself distracted by trying to make the stubborn curls fall just so. "About your gown? Should you rather wear the blue velvet?"

"What?" Carmen shook her head. "No, the aubergine satin is quite all right. I was merely wondering if I am doing the right thing in accepting Lady Elizabeth's invitation to the theater."

"You love the Shakespeare!"

"I do. But really I invited her to tea in the first place to decline her kind offer to paint my portrait. Then suddenly we were at Gunter's with Isabella, and she was saying I had to meet her husband! Then I agreed to this theater outing. I probably should have gone to Lady Wright's card party instead." Carmen's gaze dropped to the jewelry arrayed before her, her wedding ring winking amid the glittering tangle. She picked it up and slid it onto her finger. "Yet Elizabeth is so very friendly, so *persuasive*. Just as her brot . . ." Her voice faded.

Esperanza plucked up the amethyst necklace and clasped it about Carmen's throat. "I did hear that

Lady Elizabeth has a very handsome bachelor brother," she said, just as if she had read Carmen's mind. "An earl. Perhaps she is intent on a bit of matchmaking."

Carmen looked up sharply. "Where did you hear this?"

"When I took Isabella walking in the park, I met nursemaids and governesses, all of them full of silly gossip. They say every single lady in Society has set her cap for this earl. But he is called the Ice Earl, because he pays scant attention to any of them . . ."

Carmen stood abruptly and reached for her gown, pulling the rustling purple folds over her head to disguise her bewilderment. "They say no one can hold his regard?" she said, muffled.

"So they say. Here, stop that, Carmencita! You are crushing your gown." Esperanza straightened the skirt and began to fasten the tiny amethyst buttons up the back. "Though Lady Dobbin's nursemaid said that she had heard that was soon to change, so perhaps Lady Elizabeth is not trying to matchmake after all."

Carmen's hand stilled on the sleeve she was adjusting. "Change in what way?"

"She said that this earl has been seen about with a certain Lady Deidra Clearbridge, daughter of the Earl of Chiswick. I believe we met him and his countess once in Vienna."

"Yes," Carmen murmured vaguely. "Perhaps. And Elizabeth's brother is going to make an offer for his daughter?"

"So she said. But maybe you will meet him yourself tonight!"

Before Carmen could answer, the heavy knocker at the front door sounded.

"That will be Elizabeth and her husband, come to collect me," she said. "You go down and make sure that the new housemaid answers the door, Esperanza. I can finish here."

"If you are certain . . ." Esperanza doubtfully eyed Carmen's stockinged feet. Then she nodded and hurried off, Carmen's evening cloak folded over her arm.

Carmen slid her feet into her satin slippers, and clasped her gold Etruscan bracelets over her arms, hardly knowing what she was doing.

Peter *betrothed*.

It was very foolish of her to have not even considered that he might have moved on with his life, romantically speaking. It had been many years since their romance and marriage. And a handsome, wealthy earl was a catch indeed.

Yet, since she had never forgotten, she had assumed that he had not. She had had chances, many of them, to form new attachments, both respectable and decidedly not so. She had even liked some of those men very much. But none of them had been Peter. None of them, no matter how handsome or how nice, had ever made her feel that warmth, that excitement, that full-of-joy way that he had.

The way he still did, despite everything.

She held out her hand and stared down at the mesmerizing green fire of her emerald for a long moment. She had worn it every day since he had placed it there. Would she soon have to remove it forever?

"You are a fool, Carmen," she told herself. "A silly, moonstruck fool, and you are too old for this behavior."

She took up her fan and her opera glasses, and went out onto the staircase landing.

Elizabeth and her husband awaited her down in the tiny foyer, Elizabeth chattering about something as she adjusted her attire in the gold-framed mirror hanging there. She was the first to see Carmen, and waved up at her. "Hello! Are we terribly early?"

Sir Nicholas Hollingsworth looked up at her then, a charming smile of greeting on his face. The smile disappeared when he saw her, and his face, bronzed from the Italian sun, turned rather grayish.

"Hello, Nicholas," Carmen said quietly, moving slowly down the stairs. "I am not a ghost, I do assure you." She paused on the last step and looked at him. She could have wept, he seemed so very familiar and dear. Yet different, just as Peter did.

A long white scar sliced across one cheek, and he leaned heavily on a carved walking stick. The spoils of war. But there was no lurking sadness in his eyes, as there was in Peter's. How could there be, married to Elizabeth? He still appeared the lighthearted young officer who had stood witness at her wedding.

"Oh, Nick," she said. "It is so good to see you again."

He reached out one shaking hand to touch her arm. "Carmen?"

"Yes, it is I."

Suddenly he caught her in his arms and twirled her around, laughing. "By Jove, *Carmen*! I knew *you* could never be dead. You were always far too wily for those Frenchies."

When he finally placed her back on her feet, Carmen reached out to lean on the newel post, giggling dizzily. "As, I see, were you!"

Elizabeth clapped her hands happily. "I knew you would be so happy, Nick! I could scarce keep it to myself."

Nicholas threw his arm around his wife's shoulders, still grinning at Carmen. "You knew about this, Lizzie? That the condesa was Carmen?"

"Oh, yes. I knew when I met her at the Dacey ball. But I also knew that you would never believe me, that you would have to see for yourself."

"Well, well," Nicholas mused. "What an interesting tale you must have, Carmen, of the past six years."

"Indeed I do. As, I am sure, do you." The clock in the foyer chimed the hour. Carmen reached for the cloak Esperanza had left draped over a chair, and allowed Nicholas to help her don it. "But you must tell it to me in the carriage, or we shall surely be late, and *Much Ado About Nothing* is my very favorite play."

"Oh, yes!" Elizabeth cried. "You must tell her the tale of how we met, dearest. She of all people should appreciate Peter's role in it."

The theater was quite full when Carmen, Elizabeth, and Nicholas made their way into their box. The houselights had not yet been lowered, but the boxes surrounding their own were filled with the glitter of jewels and satins and inquisitive opera glasses.

Elizabeth immediately seated herself in the center of the box, and turned her glass to examining the gowns of others.

Nicholas sat next to Carmen. "Tell me what you have been doing since the war," he said. "How you came to be alive! We all thought you dead."

Carmen smiled wryly. "Yes, so I have heard! But I thought all of you dead, as well. Tell me, are any of the regiment besides you and Peter alive?"

"There is Robert Means. Do you remember him?"

"Oh, yes! Lieutenant Means," she mused. "Such a dreadful cardplayer, he owes me a veritable fortune! Or would if we had played for stakes. And he is alive, you say?"

"Should be in Town any day now. His cousin is making her bow this Season, or so I heard. Usually he stays immured at his estate in farthest Cornwall." Nicholas grinned at her. "He always did have an appreciative eye for you, Carmen! I'm certain he will be more than happy to renew the acquaintance."

Carmen smiled and blushed. "He was a sweet man, as I recall, and quite handsome. But . . ." She turned away from Nicholas's forthright gaze.

"But you never saw anyone but Peter," he said quietly. "Nor he any but you."

She raised her gaze back to his, to find his dark eyes steady and serious. "No. I never saw any but him."

"Have you—met him yet?"

"Twice. Once at the Dacey ball, where I also met your wife." Carmen glanced at Elizabeth, who was still studying the audience. More to give them a chance to speak quietly than from any genuine interest, Carmen suspected. "I also saw him this very morning, when he came to my house to return an ivory comb I had lost."

"How, if I may be so bold as to ask, did these meetings proceed?"

Carmen twirled her opera glass through her fingers, watching the light dance on the mother-of-pearl. "As well as could be expected, I suppose. He has had so many years to be angry with me. I doubt we can ever be as we were in Spain."

"He believed you were in league with Chauvin."

"Yes," Carmen sighed.

"But you were not." It was a statement rather than a question.

"Of course I was not! I was riding to fetch reinforcements when I was shot down by Chauvin. It was a miracle that I and—that I survived." And the babe inside her, as well. "I am so very happy that *you* believe me, Nick."

"How could I do otherwise? No one could have been more loyal than you, to your country *and* to your husband. I still cannot fathom that Peter would condemn you on such flimsy evidence as the fact that you were seen with Chauvin at the battle. I was wounded, and even I could see you were in a stupor."

"Then, why could Peter not see?" Carmen cried. "He is—was my husband."

"Peter is very stubborn, as you are no doubt well aware. He will not always listen to reason, as I do."

Elizabeth snorted inelegantly at that.

"As I do," Nicholas repeated loudly. "He had a very difficult time indeed when he returned from Spain. He was not at all himself for a very long time. But I am certain that, between the three of us, we can make him see sense."

"Do you think so?" Carmen whispered. "Do you really think so, Nick?"

Elizabeth gave a small gasp. "Well! Speak of the devil and he shall appear, as my old nanny always used to say."

Carmen looked over at Elizabeth, who had her glass trained on a box across the way. "What is it, Lizzie?"

She turned her own glass to the box.

And saw Peter, immaculately elegant in a deep burgundy velvet evening coat, matching brocade waistcoat, and perfectly tied snow-white cravat. His golden hair gleamed in the light.

He was not alone. He was assisting a lady into her seat. A very beautiful, very *young* lady, with red-gold curls framing a heart-shaped face. Her gown was the gown of a young girl, even, white tulle over a slip of pink silk, trimmed with tiny pink satin rosebuds.

Carmen never could abide pink.

"That looby!" Elizabeth said with a hiss. "He never said he would be here tonight, let alone that he would be escorting Lady Deidra Clearbridge and her mama."

Carmen watched the two bright heads bend together as the lady said something that made Peter smile gently.

Carmen's lips pressed together tightly. This must be the woman that Esperanza said the nursemaids giggled about. "Who is this Lady Deidra?"

Elizabeth's glass never wavered from her brother's box. "She is the youngest daughter of the Earl of Chiswick. This is her second Season, but not, from what I hear, for lack of offers. She has merely been waiting for—bigger fish." Lady Deidra laid her fan on Peter's arm, and peeked up at him from beneath her lashes. "And it appears that she thinks she has landed the largest trout of all. We shall soon see about that."

"Elizabeth," Carmen began, but she was interrupted as the curtain rose. "I don't want to cause a scene," she whispered. "Not yet, anyway."

"Quite right. Gather the troops, and all that. But in the end, Carmen, *you* are his wife, and your Isabella is his daughter. Lady Milquetoast hasn't a chance."

Nicholas, who had not heard all his wife's words but had certainly heard her tone, warned, "Lizzie . . ."

"I know, darling. I am being mean. But that Lady Deidra is completely wrong for my brother. I don't know what he could be thinking."

"That she is suitable and pretty? That it is time for him to set up his nursery, just as you have urged him?" Nicholas laughed, obviously intent on playing devil's advocate.

"If only he knew."

Nicholas threw a puzzled glance at his wife. "Knew what, dear?"

"We will tell you later," the women chorused.

As the overture finished and the actors appeared

onstage, Elizabeth leaned over and whispered in Carmen's ear. "I am having a house party next month at Evanstone Park, our new house in Derbyshire. You must come."

Carmen considered this. A quiet weekend in the country, far away from the clamor and glitter of the Season, where she could think and regroup, sounded just the thing. "I think I would enjoy that very much."

Elizabeth smiled. "I thought you might say that."

As the curtain closed for the interval, Elizabeth tapped her fan on her husband's arm. "Nick, I am quite parched. Do you think there might be some lemonade to be had? Or, better yet, champagne?"

"I shall go and see what I can find, my love," Nicholas answered.

Carmen glanced across the way where Peter and Lady Deidra Clearbridge were talking. "I know that ladies should really not go wandering about the theater, but may I come with you, Nicholas?" she said. "I find myself in need of some air."

"I shall come as well," Elizabeth said. "We shall promenade about and show off our gowns, rather than waiting for people to come to us!"

So the ladies left their box and, one on each of Nicholas's arms, made their way into the throng of the foyer in search of refreshment. Their mission successful, they ensconced themselves in a small nook to sip at their lemonade and watch the passersby.

"This must all seem very tame to you, Carmen, after the splendors of Paris and Vienna," Elizabeth commented as she waved to a diamond-draped dowager.

"Does it seem so to you, after living in Italy?" Carmen answered.

"Yes, at times. Certainly nothing can rival Venice

during Carneval for gaiety." Elizabeth smiled at her husband, soft and secret. "Can it, my dear?"

"Assuredly not."

"And, of course, there are a great many artists living there now. It is quite congenial," Elizabeth continued. "I miss my dear friend, Mrs. Georgina Beaumont, who you will perhaps have heard of. Her house is directly across the canal from ours, and she gives the loveliest parties! But then, you will meet her at our country house weekend. She is arriving in England any day."

"London will never be the same, after the havoc my wife and Georgina are sure to wreak on it!" Nicholas said with a laugh.

"I cannot wait," said Carmen.

"Shall we go back?" Nicholas asked. "I do believe the next act will be beginning directly."

No sooner had they disposed of their empty glasses and turned back toward their box when they came face-to-face with Peter.

And Lady Deidra Clearbridge, on his arm.

"Peter!" Elizabeth cried in surprise, quite as if she had not been watching them through her glass all evening. "I did not know *you* had planned a theater excursion, or we could have shared a carriage." She went up on tiptoe to kiss his cheek, and beamed from him to Carmen as if she had pulled some great coup.

Peter's gaze was steady on Carmen, his eyes calm and expressionless as blue ice. "Did I not say so, Lizzie? How remiss of me? I believe you have met Lady Deidra Clearbridge."

"Yes, of course." Elizabeth slowly held out her hand to the petite blonde. "How lovely to see you again, Lady Deidra."

"Yes," Deidra answered, her voice low and musical. "How do you do, Lady Elizabeth."

"This is Elizabeth's husband, Sir Nicholas Hollingsworth," Peter added. "And . . . the famous Condesa de Santiago."

Deidra inclined her red-gold head. "So lovely to meet both of you. And such a very pretty frock, Condesa. You must give me the name of your mantuamaker."

"Yes, of course," Carmen answered, hoping that her voice would remain steady and cool. "Your own gown is quite—delightful, Lady Deidra."

Deidra gave a small, rather tight smile. Perhaps she had read that ridiculous gossip about the Dacey ball and moonlit terraces. Confounded scandalmongers.

Elizabeth gave her brother one long, speaking look. "I think the play is about to resume. Shall we see you later at Clifton House, Peter?"

"Of course. Shall I order a cold supper?"

"No, no, we—the three of us—are going out to supper."

"Then, I shall see you tomorrow."

"Yes," Elizabeth said. "We have so much to talk about, brother dear."

Elizabeth linked one arm in Nicholas's and the other in Carmen's, and led them away from the golden pair that was watching them walk away.

Elizabeth had a very thoughtful look on her face. Carmen felt sure she should be afraid.

The house was dark and silent when Carmen arrived back in the wee hours, the merest bit unsteady on her feet after the champagne supper she had enjoyed with Nicholas and Elizabeth. One candle had been left burning on the table in the foyer, and Carmen took it up and made her way to Isabella's room.

Her daughter was sleeping curled up on her side, one tiny fist under her cheek. Her golden curls were tangled on her lace-edged pillows, and her dreams were causing a frown to mar her fair brow.

She looked so like her father when she slept, fighting battles even in slumber.

Carmen put down the candle and bent to place a careful kiss on Isabella's cheek, to smooth the curls back from her face.

Isabella stirred, blinking her brown eyes open. "Mama? Is that you?"

"Yes, darling, it is me. I'm home."

"Were you with Lady Elizabeth?"

"Yes, and her husband. Did you have a good evening with Esperanza?"

"Um-hm. We had a blanc mange for dessert. I do like Lady Elizabeth, Mama."

"I am glad you liked her, dear. She is very nice, and I am sure she liked *you* a great deal."

"I never saw a grown-up eat *three* ices before. How does she not get very fat?"

Carmen laughed. "I don't know, darling!"

"Will I see her again soon?"

"On Thursday, if you like. We are going riding in the park."

"That is very good, Mama. You need a friend."

Oh, the wisdom of the young. Carmen smiled. "You are quite right, Bella. I think Lady Elizabeth and I will be very good friends. So you shall see her on Thursday. But now you must go back to sleep."

Isabella yawned hugely in agreement. "Good night, Mama."

"Good night, *querida*."

Carmen pressed one more kiss on her daughter's soft cheek, then left, closing the door gently behind her.

Her own room was warm with a banked fire in the grate, the bedclothes turned back invitingly. Carmen sighed wearily, and went to her dressing table to remove her jewels.

Propped there against the jewel case was the afternoon post, which she had missed in the excitement of preparing for the evening. She sifted listlessly through the new invitations and letters.

Then she froze.

In her hand was a cheap envelope, addressed to her in dark block letters and sealed with that ominous black wax.

Slowly, reluctantly, she broke the seal with the back of her brooch and read the words written there.

Chapter Eight

"Should you be spending so much time with the condesa, Elizabeth?"

Peter's voice was quiet and calm as he confronted his sister, yet there was steel in his words.

Elizabeth tossed her hat and riding crop onto a library chair, and began peeling off her gloves. "Indeed?"

"People may begin to think that—well, that your friendship, along with those gossiping articles in the papers, may give the impression that there could be something between our—our families."

"Why, Peter, never say you are stammering! I believe your infamous composure is rattled." Elizabeth grinned at him. "Are you afraid that Lady Deidra may decline your attentions if there are rumors about—your family and the condesa?"

"Elizabeth . . ."

"Surely it is only proper that your sister get to know your wife."

At that, his "infamous composure" shattered entirely. He shot up from his chair, his hands planted on his desk. "How did you know . . . ? Did she say . . . ?"

"Don't be so bacon-brained! Did you not show me her miniature only last year, and tell me of your marriage in Spain? I knew her the first—well, the second moment I saw her at the Dacey ball. She is quite distinctive."

Peter slowly sat back down, and rubbed his hand across his face. "Your memory is too sharp by half, Lizzie."

"I am an artist; it is my calling to remember faces. And I do truly like Carmen, since I have had a chance to know her. She is kind and tells such funny stories. And she is a bruising rider! She quite left me, and all her admirers, in the dust at the park this afternoon. *And,* furthermore, she is quite as intelligent as she is beautiful, unlike so many of your other chosen companions, who shall remain nameless. Truly a match for you, brother. Here I thought there could never be a woman in the world who could tolerate you!"

He smiled reluctantly. "I thought we were a match once, as well. Such did not prove to be the case. Now we have moved forward with our lives."

Elizabeth studied him quietly for a long moment. Then she slowly shook her head. "You are being a fool."

"I told you what happened in Spain, Lizzie!"

"With all respect, Peter, sometimes you cannot see past the end of your nose! I do not know exactly what happened in Spain, of course, but I know that Carmen would never have played you, or anyone, false. Nicholas feels the same as I, and he was there!"

"You do not know what you are speaking of. People said . . . I saw . . ." He broke off with a soft curse. "Nicholas was always charmed by her, and now so are you."

"There is no talking to you when you are in a mood." Elizabeth gathered up the train of her riding habit. "I am going to bathe and change. We are going to Lady Carstairs's rout tonight. Will you be there?"

"I do plan to attend."

"With Lady Deidra?"

"Perhaps. Are you and Nicholas bringing Carmen?"

"Of course. We are so 'charmed' by her, we want to spend every bit of time we can with her!" She smiled sweetly. "So we shall see you there."

"May I go, Mama?" Isabella leaned against Carmen's leg as she sat at her dressing table brushing her hair, one tiny hand stroking the soft satin of Carmen's deep burgundy-red gown.

Carmen laughed. "Not tonight! You are still too young for balls, Bella. When you are all grown-up, and make your bow, we shall have the grandest, most extravagant ball anyone has ever seen."

"And I'll have a satin gown? A pink one? And diamonds?" She reached for her mother's diamond bracelet and slid it over her own arm, admiring the flash of it against her nightgown sleeve.

"Whatever you like." Carmen held a ruby and diamond drop on a gold chain up to her throat. "This one, Bella?"

Isabella cocked her little head to one side. "Yes, that is pretty."

"I think so, too." Carmen fastened the necklace about her throat and reached for the matching earrings.

"Will Lady Elizabeth come to my ball?"

"Of course she will! As will hundreds of other people, everyone we have ever met."

Isabella's gaze fell as she fidgeted with Carmen's enameled pot of rice powder. "But there won't be . . ."

"Won't be what, darling?"

"Esperanza has been reading me a book where the princess dances with her father, the king, at a ball, and then she meets Prince Charming. But I won't have a father to dance with."

Carmen looked down at her daughter in shock. She put her arm about her and hugged her close. "Oh, Bella! I am certain that there will be many, many men to dance with you at every ball you ever attend, including a Prince Charming."

Isabella smiled, but it was rather watery. "Yes, of course." The knocker on the front door sounded, and she brightened. "That's Lady Elizabeth! May I go down and say hello, Mama? She promised to come in and say hello to me specially."

"Yes, of course, dear, if you will give me my bracelet back. Tell her I will be down directly."

Carmen watched Isabella scamper away before she let her smile fade.

Isabella had very seldom asked about her father. She had always been so content with Carmen's brief explanation that her father had been a very brave man who had died in the war, and gone to heaven when Isabella was very small. And, despite a small wistfulness on the very few occasions Carmen had allowed a gentleman to come to their house to escort her to a party, Isabella had seemed entirely content to have her mother to herself.

Whatever could have brought on such questions now? Could it be only the book that Esperanza was reading to her?

Carmen only hoped that Esperanza was not putting too many ideas into Isabella's head with those fairy stories. Kings did not suddenly appear on white horses to set princesses lives aright in one fell swoop, after all. As Carmen herself well knew.

The Carstairs rout was not the dreadful crush the Dacey ball had been, but carriages were still lined up around the street, waiting to disgorge their passengers. A few people, in their silks and jewels, had become impatient and were now walking along the pavement to the front doors.

Carmen watched these pedestrians from her carriage window, fidgeting with the tiny buttons on her gloves. She was almost tempted to claim a megrim and ask the Hollingsworths to take her back home. It was sure to be a long, trying evening.

She knew, though, that Elizabeth would guess right away that Carmen was afraid of encountering Peter and his Lady Deidra again. It would be just too humiliating for her cowardice to be so exposed!

So she adjusted the small, burgundy-colored satin turban, fastened with a ruby brooch, that held her hair in place, and smiled brightly at Elizabeth and Nicholas.

Elizabeth beamed in return. She had been quite uncharacteristically quiet on the short drive, occasionally tapping one finger against her chin thoughtfully.

She reminded Carmen of Isabella, when she was plotting some mischief.

But all Elizabeth did was dig about in her reticule and come up with a letter, which she handed over to Carmen. "I have such a surprise for you!"

"A surprise?" Carmen looked down suspiciously at the paper. "What is it?"

"Just read it. It is not a snake; it will not bite you."

Carmen slowly unfolded it. "A voucher to Almack's?"

Elizabeth laughed and clapped her hands. "Isn't it too grand? I painted Lady Castlereagh's portrait last year, and she was very pleased with it. She was more than happy to give you a voucher. We can go the Wednesday after we return from the country."

"Oh, Lizzie!" Carmen giggled at the thought of a dull, socially correct evening at Almack's. Would she have to wear white? "Whyever would I want to go to Almack's? I am no young miss trying to snare a husband! I hear that the refreshments are abominable."

Elizabeth shrugged. "Perhaps. But then, a voucher to Almack's is essential to getting along in Society— even for a countess. It gives one such an air of respectability. And you never know who you will encounter there."

"You are up to something, Lizzie," Nicholas said sternly.

"I certainly am not! I am up to nothing but doing a small favor for a friend."

Carmen tucked the voucher away. "Well, thank you, Lizzie. I shall certainly go to Almack's with you, as you have been such a fine friend to me. If I am still in England then."

Elizabeth looked at her sharply. "Still in England? Never say you are planning to leave us already? I have so many plans!"

"I do not know. I have learned never to set definite plans in my life. They always seem to end up changing."

"But you cannot . . ." Elizabeth began.

Nicholas laid his hand on her arm. "Now, dearest, if you hound Carmen, she is sure to leave us! You must allow her, and Peter, to find their own way."

His voice was low, meant only for his wife's ears, but Carmen heard him still. She turned away, blushing.

She had not blushed since she was a schoolgirl, at the Carmelite convent, whispering with her friend Elena Granjero. That had been many, many years ago, and yet now she so often felt the telltale warmth in her cheeks again!

"Oh, look!" she cried in relief as the carriage halted at the doors. "We have arrived at last."

The dancing had already begun by the time they

made their way through the receiving line, and a stately pavane was forming on the dance floor. The crowd was of a goodly size, but the hum of conversation was still low.

"I do hope we can liven things up," Elizabeth said. "Or I will have wasted a new gown on a very dull evening!"

"A new gown is *never* wasted," Carmen answered. "Nicholas shall have to bribe the orchestra to play a waltz, and the two of you can scandalize everyone by dancing far too close. Perhaps you could even kiss!"

Elizabeth shook her head. " 'Tis no good! We are an old married couple, and no one is shocked by what we do any longer. We shall have to find someone for *you* to waltz with."

"Such as who?" Carmen laughed. "Lord Stonehurst, perhaps?" She gestured with her closed fan to the portly little marquis, who was trying to wink at her in an alluring fashion. He looked a bit like a fish.

"Certainly not! The old hedgehog. He would never suit our purposes."

"Oh? And what are 'our' purposes?"

"To make certain parties sick with jealousy, of course."

The pavane ended, and sets began to form for a country-dance. Nicholas held out his arm to his wife. "Come, my love," he said. "Dance with me, and let Carmen rest from all your scheming."

Elizabeth rolled her eyes in exasperation, but allowed him to lead her away.

Carmen waved them off, then looked about for acquaintances she should greet.

Her searching gaze fell on Peter, who had just entered the ballroom and stood conversing with a small group.

And Lady Deidra on his arm. With rather too much bosom showing in her white satin gown for such a *young* woman. Surely her mother, who stood nearby like a great battleship in gray silk, should have prevented her from so exposing herself.

Peter looked up then and caught Carmen staring at him. One corner at his lips quirked up, as if to smile at her.

Or as if to mock her sour thoughts.

She tilted up her chin and looked away. But it was almost as if she could still feel his gaze on her, warm against her skin.

She drew her fur-edged satin shawl closer about her shoulders.

"Carmen?" a quiet, incredulous voice said from behind her. "Carmen Montero?"

She looked over her shoulder to see a tall, handsome man with red, curling hair and wide green eyes. His face was a ghostly white as he looked at her.

She was becoming so familiar with that expression on people's faces as they looked at her. But this was a particularly welcome face.

"Robert Means!" she cried in delight. "How utterly wonderful to see you. Nicholas told me that you were in England, but that you seldom came to Town." She held out her hand to him.

He took it between both of his, holding it very tightly. "I don't, but I am very glad to be here now! Oh, Carmen, I never expected to see you again this side of the hereafter."

"Nor I you. Not after the battle we saw! But come, walk with me. Tell me what you have been doing all these years."

Robert offered her his arm. "Only if *you* will tell me all of what you have been doing. I am sure it must be more exciting than my tales of the wilds of Cornwall."

"I am certain not! Are you still a wicked cardplayer?"

"When I get the chance of it. There is little society where I live."

"But more than in Spain, I am certain!" Carmen smiled at him.

"Perhaps a tad more variety than in Spain, true!" he answered with a laugh. "But I had *your* society in Spain. That quite made up for any discomforts. I have thought of you so often over the years."

Carmen was not at all certain she was happy with the direction of their conversation.

She liked Robert Means; she always had. But she had always had the uncomfortable sense that his feelings for her went beyond friendship.

She had quite forgotten that, until now, with his warm gaze and soft smile on her.

She laughed lightly and tapped his arm with her fan. "I have thought of you, as well. But you cannot deny that there must be some pretty girl for you in Cornwall! You have always been far too nice to remain a bachelor."

He shook his head. "There was some talk in my family of a match with my cousin." He nodded toward a young brunette in pink silk across the room. "But we did not suit. I am afraid, Carmen, that I gave my heart away years ago, and there has been no one to compare since."

Carmen swallowed hard, her mouth suddenly dry. She forced another light laugh. "Oh, Robert! We should not be so serious at such a merry party."

He laughed ruefully. "How very right you are! Shall we dance instead?"

"Oh, yes. Let's."

Peter watched with narrowed eyes the progress of Carmen and Robert Means around the room.

Robert Means, of all people! Robert, the man who . . .

Robert had always proclaimed his love for Carmen, to Carmen herself, to any of the regiment who would listen. Indeed, Peter had once thought Robert as devastated by Carmen's betrayal as Peter himself was. He had thought that to be the reason Robert had buried himself in Cornwall.

Now, as he watched Robert laugh with Carmen, saw the light of avarice and lust in those green eyes, he knew that Robert's feelings did not come from love, but from a very deep hatred. For Carmen, perhaps, yet most assuredly for Peter. He could not say from whence it sprang. Was it jealousy?

Whatever it had been, and was, Peter knew one thing for very certain. He could not bear to leave Carmen in Robert's presence for an instant longer.

Carmen laughed at something Robert said to her, her dark head tilted back to reveal her swan-like throat. Peter remembered how he had loved to slide his arms around her waist and bend his head to nuzzle at that creamy skin. She had always smelled of jasmine, and sunshine . . .

His hand tightened on the champagne glass in his hand. Those days were long past, and if she wished to flirt with that bedamned Robert Means, or anyone else, then why should he even care.

Yet he did. He cared very much.

If only he could speak with her alone again, and discover what had truly happened in Spain and during her life after. Then perhaps he could cease thinking of her day and night. Cease pondering what she might be doing when he was meant to be going over estate accounts, or taking Lady Deidra driving in the park.

Lady Deidra.

She tugged lightly on his sleeve then, drawing his gaze away from Carmen and her attentive escort.

"Do you not agree, Lord Clifton?" she said, her voice soft and sweet. Her blue eyes gazed up at him steadily, a bit vacantly.

Such English eyes, pale and modest, framed in yellow lashes. They did not flash and fire like darker eyes, speaking of warm nights and fragrant gardens.

Peter pushed away such thoughts, and looked around at the small group they were conversing with. Political men from his club, and their proper wives. They all watched him expectantly.

"Oh, yes," he said. "Quite."

Apparently that was the correct answer, for Deidra smiled at him and nodded. The hum of conversation resumed around him, and he looked out at the ballroom again.

Carmen and Robert were still walking about the periphery of the party, their faces smiling as they spoke quietly together. As he watched, they turned their steps toward the dancing.

He felt his resolve to remove her from Robert's somehow-poisonous presence strengthen.

"Would you care for some punch, Lady Deidra?" he said, interrupting whatever old Lord Pinchon was saying.

She blinked up at him. "Why—yes. Some punch would be lovely. Is everything quite all right, Lord Clifton?"

"Yes, certainly. Now, if you will excuse me . . ."

As he moved away, Lady Deidra watched him for a moment, then turned her attention back to the conversation, nodding and asking Lord Pinchon a question.

She was so very poised, the perfect, polished political hostess.

Now, where the devil was Carmen?

Then he saw her, dancing now with Robert. Her tall, slim figure swirled through the figures, gracefully dipping and swaying as Robert twirled her about. Her slippers seemed to fly, barely touching the parquet floor. She laughed up at her partner, her face alight.

The sophisticated countess had vanished, and here was *his* Carmen again. The brave, laughing girl who had loved to dance around campfires, who he had kissed under Spanish stars and held in his arms.

Made love to.

The music ended, quite startling Peter, who had not realized he had spent so many minutes staring. Carmen was leaving the dance floor on Robert's arm.

Peter thrust his empty glass at a passing footman, and strode across the floor. He did not even see the many pairs of eyes that watched him with great interest, including those of Lady Deidra and her mother.

He halted at where Carmen stood, Robert Means's arm linked in hers.

"Condesa," he said quietly. "Dance with me."

Carmen gaped up at Peter. The music was beginning again, couples moving past them, but all she could see was him.

All she heard were his words, not the whispers and giggles of the other guests.

She closed her eyes tightly, and those words echoed in her mind. *Dance with me . . .*

"Dance with me, Carmen!"

She laughed up at her major. "You are moon-mad, Major Everdean! How can we dance here? Outdoors . . . with no music? And I am not wearing my ball gown!"

She pirouetted about in her trousers and boots.

"Can you not hear it?" His face, golden with the touch of sunlight, was merry as he looked down at her. The lines about his eyes deep with a smile.

"Hear what?"

"The music, of course. I believe it is a waltz."

Carmen heard only the rush of the river they were strolling beside, the sounds of voices and laughter from the nearby encampment. But she cocked her head to one side, pretending to hear the lilting notes. "I do believe you are correct, querido! A waltz, indeed."

He held out his hand. "So—will you dance with me, Carmen?"

"I would be honored, Peter." She dipped into an elaborate court curtsy, as if she wore the grandest satin ball gown and diamonds.

Then Peter swung her in a wide arc, his hand warm at her waist. They were much closer than would ever be proper in a fine ballroom; her very traditional mother would have fainted, had she been alive to see! Carmen cared not a whit. Peter whirled her around, around, until the sky tilted above them, and she leaned her forehead against his shoulder and laughed until she cried . . .

Carmen blinked quickly, back suddenly from her sunny riverback. Peter stood before her, not the dashing English officer who had waltzed with her beneath the branches of trees, but unsmiling and stern. His red coat was gone, replaced with elegant but austere dark green superfine.

This man would not dance with her on a grassy floor until she was dizzy with love and laughter and blossoming love and they collapsed, breathless, onto the ground.

She looked at him now, and saw all that she lost since that magical day. She burst into tears, breaking away from Robert and fleeing the ballroom. The crowd parted before her in utter silence, entranced by the possibility of a scene in their midst.

Peter moved not at all, staring directly before him, until he turned on his heel and left the room in her wake. He hurried past the gawking crowd, the footmen at the front doors, onto the pavement outside the Carstairs's house. But Carmen had vanished.

The street was quiet, except for rows of carriages waiting for the ball to cease and their owners to return.

Then he heard the faint click of shoe heels on pavement. He turned and saw a fur-trimmed burgundy satin train disappearing around a corner.

He dashed off down the street, calling after her. "Carmen! Carmen, please wait."

When he came around the corner after her, he found that she had halted at his cry, but had not turned back. She stood there on the pavement, one hand on the wrought-iron railings of a fence. Her shoulders shook a bit, as if she were breathing too deeply, but otherwise she was completely still.

Peter had the sudden, powerful urge to kiss the pale, vulnerable nape of her neck, exposed by her new cropped coiffure.

"Carmen," he said. "Why did you run away?"

"Why did you follow me?" she answered.

"Well, I . . ." Peter paused. Why *had* he run after her so impulsively? "I wanted to apologize."

"For asking me to dance?"

"It seemed to embarrass you. Perhaps you simply could not bring yourself to dance with the likes of me."

She turned around. Her eyes seemed too bright, but she was composed. "It would only do my reputation good and no ill to be seen dancing with the famous Ice Earl, aside from those silly gossipy articles. And, if you are as fine a dancer as you once were, I am sure it would have been most enjoyable."

"Then, why did you leave?" Peter was baffled.

"I was—startled."

"Startled?"

"Yes. That you would ask me to dance, a woman you dislike so. I suppose I questioned your motives."

"My motives were only to dance with you!" And to separate her from Robert Means. "To speak with you."

"Indeed?"

"Indeed. I have many questions I would like to ask you."

"I am here now. Ask me, Peter."

Peter looked about. The street they were standing on, wide and well lit, faced a small square where there were several benches. "We cannot talk standing here."

"I do not wish to return to the ball. No doubt it is buzzing with speculation."

"Then, will you sit with me over in that square? Just for a moment. When you are feeling more the thing, we can return to the ball. Or I can see you home."

Carmen glanced uncertainly at the square. "Are you sure it will be safe?"

"Carmen, you will be much safer sitting there with me than wandering the streets of London alone."

She nodded. "Of course. Yes, I will sit with you for a moment."

"Thank you." Peter took her arm to lead her across the street. There was a small patch of skin below her sleeve and above her glove that was bare, and that was where his hand fell. It was almost a shock to feel his palm against her warm flesh. It was as soft as velvet, just as he remembered that once all her body had been.

Once her hair had been long and had cloaked her sun-golden, soft nakedness like a shining black curtain, as she leaned forward to kiss him . . .

His hand jerked on her arm.

She turned her head to look at him. "Peter?"

He drew his coat closer about him, hoping it was too dark for her to see the new fullness at the front of his close-fitting trousers. "Shall we sit here?"

"Yes, certainly."

Carmen looked up at Peter as she settled herself on the bench, puzzled. He seemed so—discomposed suddenly. Almost as much as she was. "What did you wish to talk about?"

His eyes were wide as he looked down at her, almost as if he were rather startled to find her there. "What?"

"You asked me to dance because you wished to speak with me. I merely inquired what about. After all, when you came to call on me at my house, you seemed to have everything settled about me in your mind."

"No more than you have about me!" he snapped.

"I beg your pardon? I did not hurl accusations at *you*."

"No. You just think me capable of being cruel and close-minded. You think me bitter and implacable."

Carmen rather felt that was the gist of it. "Did you not accuse me of spying against your regiment?"

"Yes, of course. But—no." He shook his head. "Forgive me, Carmen. I am rather confused."

"Well, that makes two of us. I have been utterly bewildered ever since I saw you again."

Peter drew in a deep breath. "It is true that I have buried myself in regrets these past years. I did think those things of you, on the evidence I had at hand."

"The flimsy evidence of seeing me with Chauvin!"

"That, and—other things." But he did not want to bring Robert Means into it just at present. He only wanted Carmen to understand his own feelings. "Yes, flimsy evidence, as you say. But as the years passed, I clung to my anger, and it grew. Anger was so much preferable to grief." He laid his hand, very gently and tentatively, against her own. "Now, as I see you again, I remember other things."

"Things such as what?"

"How very brave you were. How outspoken, how valiant. How you made me laugh, made me want to dance, when it seemed I would never want those things again." His hand moved on hers, his fingers curling beneath her palm. "What a grand kisser you were."

Carmen gave a choked laugh. "Oh, Peter!"

"It is true that you were! Why, I recall that afternoon we went walking beside what you called a river, but what was really only a small creek . . ." He broke off and stared at her. "That was it, was it not? When I asked you to dance, you thought of that afternoon."

"Yes. I remembered how very happy we were that day, and how our lives have changed since then. I was—overcome."

"I remember that day, too."

"Do you?"

Their gazes met, clung, and a silence, deeper than words, fell around them.

Then a carriage clattered past in the street. Carmen pulled away from him and rose to her feet. "We should go back. It will already be a great *on-dit* that we are both missing, and Elizabeth will be looking for me."

Peter stood beside her. "Yes. Of course. But I still have so many questions, Carmen."

She was walking away from him, her train now caught up and tossed over her arm. "As do I," she called. "I am sure we will meet again, Peter. And then all questions will be answered."

Carmen shut her bedroom door firmly, and leaned back against the solid wood. Her ribs ached from her swift run up the stairs to the safety of her room, and something that felt suspiciously like tears was making her cheeks damp.

She wiped at them impatiently with her gloved hand, then tossed her wrap and reticule onto the turned-down bed. As she stripped off her gloves, she noticed that somewhere she had lost her painted silk fan. It seemed she was losing bits of apparel every time she went out in public, first her comb and now her fan. And not even for interesting, amorous causes.

"Ah, Peter," she sighed.

She sat down at her dressing table, and rested her chin in her hand. In the glass, she appeared a disgruntled, rumpled-haired schoolgirl, with an unflattering frown on her face.

Peter was as much a puzzle as he had ever been. Did he hate her? Or did he—and this was the truly frightening thought—love her still, deep in his heart?

As she still loved him. So very much.

There. She had thought it. She loved him.

She shook her head fiercely, and sat up straighter. There was nothing she could do about Peter, or her feelings for him, that night. A better subject to occupy her mind was her own silly behavior.

"What a nodcock you were!" she told her reflection sternly. "Dashing out of there simply because he asked you to dance. What were you thinking? Do you want to cause a scandal?"

And she had been having such a productive evening with Robert Means. Robert, so open, artless, and charming. So very happy to see her again.

He had been such an unlikely soldier all those years ago; more a gentleman farmer than a warrior. He seemed an unlikely blackmailer now. Yet Carmen had learned, in very difficult and painful ways, that the way things *seemed* were so often not how they were.

Robert could very well be her letter writer. He knew of her activities in wartime; now he knew of her new place in Society. He was really her most likely candidate, as painful as that was to confess. But she would need more time to be sure.

Elizabeth's house party would be the perfect chance to become better acquainted with Robert Means. She would have to be sure he received an invitation.

Carmen's bedroom door opened, interrupting her thoughts. A tiny, white night-gowned figure appeared there, clutching a favorite doll with one hand and rubbing sleepily at her eyes with the other.

Carmen smiled at Isabella, and held out her hand. "What is it, darling? Could you not sleep?"

"I had a bad dream. I was going to find Esperanza, but I saw your light." Isabella glanced speculatively at the bed. "Could I sleep with you, Mama? Just for tonight?"

"Of course you may! Come to Mama, and tell her all about your dream." Isabella rushed into her arms then, and Carmen pressed kisses to her daughter's sleep-warm curls. Spies and blackmailers were completely forgotten. "Telling about it makes it disappear . . ."

Chapter Nine

"Well, you certainly jumped into the scandal broth last night, brother." Elizabeth stood before him, her face fierce and frowning in the harsh morning sunlight that flooded from the high library windows.

"Not now, Elizabeth," Peter bit out.

"Yes, now! Whatever were you thinking? It is not at all like you to behave so—so improperly. Embarrassing Carmen in front of everyone! Tell me what you were thinking."

"I was not thinking."

Elizabeth snorted. "That is obvious! I do not rightly understand you. You say you want nothing to do with her, that you have made a new life, then you accost her on the dance floor and cause quite an *on-dit*. Have you read the papers this morning? Are you trying to drive her back to the Continent? Do you love her, or do you not?"

"I—do not know," he said quietly.

Elizabeth shook her head at him. "Oh, Peter. Of course you know. You love her, despite everything. Just as I love Nicholas."

"But the past . . ."

"Bother the past! If I can move beyond what happened when I first met Nick, then you can surely find a way to be with the woman you love." She smoothed her hair back into its neat coiffure and tucked her shawl about her shoulders, her mind obviously now spoken. "I must go and finish packing for the journey to the country. We will see you this weekend at Evanstone Park, will we not?"

"Will Carmen be there?"

"Of course!" she answered blithely. "As will Lady Deidra Clearbridge and her *dear* mother. I received their note just yesterday."

Two days after the disastrous Carstairs rout, Robert Means came to call on Carmen.

Unfortunately, despite his cheering presence and conversation, Carmen was still distracted over her moonlit conversation with Peter.

What could it all mean, his sudden desire for peace between them? Could it mean he was at last willing to listen to her account of what had occurred in Spain? Did he merely wish to wed his proper Lady Deidra, without the dark cloud of his hasty marriage hovering over him?

Or did he desire that they be friends again? Or, perhaps, more than friends? And what did she feel about that?

Hm.

"Carmen," Robert said. Then, louder, "Condesa!"

She snapped her gaze back to him and smiled. "Yes?"

He shook his head ruefully. "You have not attended a word I have been saying."

"Indeed I have!"

"Then why, just now when I mentioned an orphanage my mother is sponsoring in Cornwall, did you smile?"

"Oh, Robert. I am sorry. I have been so tired these last days, so—distracted, by many things."

"Yes." He looked away from her, to the fire that was crackling in her drawing room grate, and to the mantel above it, crowded with many objects and pictures. "And I believe I could say what one of the chief distractions could be."

The blackmailing letters? Carmen leaned toward him. "Yes? And what is that?"

"Your husband."

"Oh." The word seemed to strike her physically, and she leaned back in her chair. "Yes, it has been rather a shock to find him suddenly in my life again, after so many years."

"You still love him, do you not?"

"I—oh, Robert, really!" she protested.

"Forgive my informality. I still find it difficult to remember that I am no longer in an army billet! Especially with old friends such as you."

"I sometimes have the same problem. And, yes—I do still love Peter." And what a relief it was, to finally say it aloud.

"Does he love you?"

Carmen shrugged. "Perhaps not. We *have* been apart a long time."

"I doubt that very much. That he does not love you, that is. How could he not?"

"Do you really think so, Robert?"

"I do." His voice hardened just a bit, and he would not meet her eyes. "I never saw a man so in love as Peter was—is with you. We seldom saw each other when we returned from Spain, but I did hear that he was not doing well at all. I knew it was hopeless mourning."

Carmen could feel the hot pricking of tears behind her eyes, and she blinked very hard to hold them back. It would never do for her to suddenly become a watering pot, especially in front of someone she was not entirely certain of. "I mourned, as well. But that was a long time ago; Peter has a new life now. As do I."

"Now, that I do not believe." Robert still would not look at her directly, but he smiled. "I will confess, Carmen, that when we met again, I cherished a few hopes of my own."

"Robert!"

"Yes. I so admired you in Spain. I had never met anyone like you. Then I saw you again, here in England, and I thought perhaps . . ." He broke off on a short bark of laughter. "Now I see I was mistaken."

Carmen reached over and patted his hand gently. "You are a dear man, Robert. I am sure you will find happiness very soon, with a very proper English miss!"

He shook his head. "Such as Lady Deidra Clearbridge, mayhap?"

Carmen laughed. "How very convenient that would be! If only you could be so obliging, Robert."

"I am not certain even I could be so obliging, Carmen."

"Well, Elizabeth kindly obtained vouchers to Almack's for us. I am sure she could do the same for you, and then we could look over the newest crop of young misses and find you a lovely one."

"I will look forward to it. But now, I must be going."

"Of course. It was so kind of you to call. And I am sure we shall see more of each other in the future."

Robert bowed over her hand, lingering just an instant more than was proper. "I am sure we shall. Good day, Carmen."

"Good day, Robert." And she watched him leave, more puzzled than ever before.

But she did not have time that day to sit and ponder over Robert Means, and whether or not he could be the blackmailer or was just a lovestruck swain. She had packing to do.

*   *   *

Carmen carefully folded a soft Indian shawl and laid it atop the gowns already in her trunk. "I do believe that is everything I shall need."

Esperanza handed her a pair of satin dancing slippers. "You forgot these, Carmencita."

Carmen groaned. "Dancing! I do not think I'll want to do very much of that this weekend."

"You love to dance!" Esperanza's tone conveyed that she did not exactly approve of *dancing*, not for proper widowed ladies anyway.

"Yes, of course I do." She slid the shoes into the trunk, and shut the lid with a bang. "Under the right circumstances."

"Isabella is very disappointed not to be going to Lady Elizabeth's party."

Carmen sighed. "Yes, I know. She was inconsolable. But I told her there would be no other children there, and she would be very bored." She sat down at her dressing table and picked up a hairbrush, only to put it back down again. Her hands simply would not be still. "Do *you* mind staying in Town alone for a few days, Esperanza?"

Esperanza shook her head. "Not a bit! The little one and I will have a splendid time. I have promised her we could have ices at Gunter's again, and go to that Astley's you told her about."

"She will adore that!" Carmen picked up the brush again and ran it quickly through her hair. "I simply could not take her with me this time."

Peter was sure to be there, and she was not at all prepared to tell Isabella's father of her existence, even though she knew it would have to be done. If only she could be certain of Peter's reaction . . .

One day she would tell him. Just not yet.

"Pardon me, Condesa."

Carmen looked up to find Rose, their new housemaid, standing in the doorway, her arms filled with flowers. "What is it, Rose?"

"These just came for you, Condesa."

"Thank you. Just put them down by the bed."

There were two bouquets: one a large mass of deep red roses, one a posy of lilies in a delicate silver filigree holder. Carmen plucked the note from the roses.

"They are from Robert Means," she told Esperanza. "How very sweet!" Such a gentleman, even after a rebuff.

She placed the card down carefully on her dressing table, eyeing the looped handwriting thoughtfully. Robert did seem so very guileless, so full of admiration for her . . .

"Well?" Esperanza said, her voice impatient.

"Well, what?"

"Who are the others from?"

Carmen put aside the roses and reached for the other note.

The words were scrawled across the paper, bold and black. "I must speak with you—Peter."

"Rose," she said, not lifting her gaze from the note. "Can you have the footman take a message to Clifton House for me?"

"Yes, of course, Condesa."

"Have him tell the earl I will meet him at three o'clock in Green Park."

Chapter Ten

Peter saw her before she saw him, and he pulled his horse up, hidden behind a tree, to watch her.

She was perched sidesaddle on her gray mare, graceful in a deep purple velvet habit. Her face was half hidden by the small net veil of her tall-crowned hat, but she was smiling as she watched a group of children frolicking.

Peter remembered then the first time he had ever seen her. She had ridden her horse hell-for-leather through their encampment in the middle of a quiet afternoon, the plumes on her outrageous, wide-brimmed green hat flying. Never had he seen anyone more dazzlingly *alive*.

He had thought on the night he married her that no woman could ever be more lovely. Yet he had been wrong, because the years had only made Carmen more beautiful. More elegant, more alive.

She looked up then, and found him watching her. At first her gloved grip tightened on the reins, and he feared she would flee before he said what he had come to say. Then she raised one hand and beckoned him nearer.

"Hello, Peter," she said quietly as he drew up beside her.

"Hello, Carmen."

"I was rather surprised to receive your flowers and your note."

"I wanted to apologize," he said, watching her hands as she fidgeted with the reins.

"What? The famous Ice Earl is apologizing yet again?" She laughed. "Whatever for?"

"For my behavior at the Carstairs rout, of course. Causing such a ridiculous scene. It is not at all like me; I cannot fathom what came over me."

"No, it is not like you. But then, we find ourselves in such a very unusual situation. I am not at all certain what the proper behavior should be."

"Quite right. But Elizabeth has been at great pains to point out how foolish I have been. I have been rude to you, have endured sleepless nights trying to think what could have gone wrong all those years ago. Then I realized that Elizabeth's advice that I simply *ask* you makes a great deal of sense."

Carmen's dark gaze was wide and unwavering behind the veil. "So that is why you asked me to meet you? To ask me what happened?"

"Of course. What else could it be?"

"I—well, I thought you were here to obtain an annulment."

"An *annulment*?"

"Yes. In order to make a proper offer to Lady Deidra. It would be quite the scandal if the Earl of Clifton was discovered to be a bigamist, yes? And divorce is so protracted."

To his great horror, Peter felt a flush spreading across his face. He coughed and looked away from her steady regard. "Er, well, we should take things one step at a time, don't you think?"

"Certainly."

"And I think the first step ought to be a clearing of the air between us. We must let the past go before we can truly look to the future."

"Yes," she murmured. "The future. We cannot speak properly here, though."

He almost expected her to invite him to her town house, but she fell silent. "Would you care to come to Clifton House? Elizabeth has gone out shopping with her friend Georgina Beaumont, so we can talk quietly."

"I think that would be best."

Carmen was not exactly sure what she had been expecting of a house with such a grand name as Clifton House. Marble halls and gilded ceilings, perhaps. Yet what she found instead was a house she herself might have decorated and lived in.

It was large to be sure, but there was no gilding and very little marble. Instead, the floors were brightly polished parquet, overlaid with brilliant red and blue Persian rugs. The furnishings in the vast foyer were heavy carved medieval pieces. A large oversize Velazquez painting hung on the wall, no doubt a souvenir from the war. There were no dainty little gold and satin Parisian chairs, or Dresden shepherdesses.

She could almost have thought herself home again.

"Your home is lovely," she said as he led her down a small hall into his book-lined library.

"You sound surprised, as if you expected me to live in some dusty mausoleum of an ancestral pile." He held out a chair for her beside the fireplace.

"I am not surprised." Her gaze went to the portrait of Peter that hung above the mantel; it was a wonderful painting, completely lifelike, to the very glow in the ice-blue eyes. "Is that one of Elizabeth's works?"

"Indeed it is."

"She is very talented."

"My sister is the finest portraitist in England," he answered with a note of rare pride in his voice.

"Would you care for some sherry, Carmen? I have some particularly fine Amontillado."

She smiled. "You remember."

"Of course I remember you like sherry. Very dry, right?" He poured some of the brownish-red liquid into a crystal goblet and pressed it into her hands. "But then, I remember many things about you, Carmen."

She took a long sip of the sherry, relishing the warm bite of it at the back of her throat. She had a feeling she was going to be in great need of it for the afternoon ahead.

"So," she said, "you wish to know what happened in Spain, on the day we parted?"

"Please."

She looked up at him, at his serious, beautiful face. "Then, I will tell you. And after, you can believe what you will. You will know the truth—all of it."

Then she put aside her glass, folded her hands in her lap, closed her eyes, and told him the whole sorry tale of her capture by Chauvin. Of being shot and tortured. Of how she in turn killed Chauvin, and made her escape.

She relived every bit of the pain and despair of that dark afternoon.

She fell silent when her tale ended; she stared down at her hands, so neatly folded in her lap, and tried not to break down in helpless sobs. She had not thought of that time in a very long while; it had been almost the worst day of her life, and she had never, ever wanted to think of it, let alone speak of it, again.

The very worst had been that day, weeks after she had fled the French encampment, when she had stumbled into a hospital and discovered that her husband was dead. Then all the pride, all the fortitude that had kept her moving forward, had quite broken down, and she had almost wished that Chauvin had killed *her*.

If she had not carried Isabella, the most precious gift, inside her, she did not know what she would have done.

Only when she was very certain that she would not start crying, did she open her eyes and look up at Peter.

He stared out of the window, half facing away from her as he watched the street below. What she could see of his face was expressionless, as pale and perfect and composed as a Renaissance statue.

The faint, very faint hope that Carmen had allowed herself to feel, the hope that he would believe her and all would be right again, now tasted like cold ashes in her mouth. There was too much time, too much anger between them. They could never again be the couple who danced on riverbanks, made love on army cots.

She had known, of course, that those days could never return. But she had harbored the hope, so very deep inside that she had not even known it until now, that the people they had become could find a common ground. A place to begin again.

Now, in the face of his silence, that hope faded.

She schooled her own features into a careful, almost mocking smoothness, and reached for her gloves.

"Well," she said, rising to her feet. She was not at all certain her shaking legs could support her, but, through willpower, they did. She lowered the veil of her hat to cover her face again. "I will incommode you no longer, my lord. I certainly did not mean to bore you with my long tale."

"I looked for you."

His voice, low and thick, stopped her from leaving the room as she intended. She looked back at him, the sunlit room now hazy behind the veil. "What did you say?"

"I looked for you, after I recovered from my wound. I was meant to be invalided home to England, but I had to go back and see what had become of you."

He looked at her, piercing her with pale blue eyes that were now nothing like ice. They were pure blue flame.

Carmen fell back onto her chair. "What did you find?"

"I found the priest who had married us. He was the only person left within miles. He told me that the remains of the French regiment had been ambushed, wiped out by partisans after a Spanish woman died there. A Spanish noblewoman." His hands fisted on the window sash, his knuckles white. His gaze never wavered from her face. "You, I thought."

Carmen pressed her hand to her mouth. She had not known, had not wanted to know what occurred at Alvaro after she had left there.

"You did not know," Peter said.

"No. I went home to Seville. I was ill, I needed to recover." To give birth. "Then, when the war was over, I left Spain and began my travels. I could no longer bear the memories of my home."

"Did you find what you searched for on those travels?"

Carmen shrugged. "Not yet. But I do have one thing I would like to ask you, Peter."

"What is that?"

She pushed back her veil, and looked him full in the face. "If the Spanish partisans did not believe me to be in league with the French, and indeed sought vengeance for my death, then why did you?"

He came and sat down in the chair across from her, his golden hair haloed in the setting sun. "The fact that I saw you riding away with Chauvin was not the only evidence I had of treachery, Carmen," he said quietly.

"What else could there possibly have been?"

"Someone told me that you had—had been Chauvin's lover in Seville, that you had shared secrets with him, news of the British Army." His gaze fell away from her in shame. "I was drunk, grief-stricken. I fear I believed it true, and went on believing it for all these years."

Carmen's chalk-white fingers clutched at the arms of her chair. She shook her head, disbelieving. "Who? Who told you such vile lies?"

"It was—Robert Means," Peter whispered.

Carmen's jaw sagged. She fell back against the chair, no longer able to remain upright. "Robert? How can that be? He just called on me this morning, to express his—admiration. Why should he do such a thing?"

"I could not say. Jealousy, perhaps."

"Jealousy?"

"That you loved me, and not him, I suppose."

"But what proof did he present?"

"He had recently been to Seville. He said he had heard it from a friend of yours, Elena, oh, I cannot recall . . ."

Carmen's jaw tightened. "Granjero. Elena Granjero."

"Yes. He said she was your best friend, that she had told him because she so hated the French."

"Ha!" Carmen laughed humorlessly. "Elena did not have two thoughts to put together in her head. She thought the French so dashing in their blue uniforms. Oh, we were friends at school, but we hardly spoke after the French invaded Spain." She drummed her fingers on the arm of her chair, her mind racing with the thought of all the treachery that had surrounded her.

Yet even as she shook her head in disbelief, she could see the awful logic of it. A girl with no conscience who had been jealous of Carmen's young marriage to the Conde de Santiago, and a man jealous of her love for Peter.

She berated herself roundly for her utter lack of suspicion, her blindness—*she*, who had built her life on correct judgment of the motives of others had not seen Robert Mean's perfidy at all.

And it had cost her greatly.

In the silence that followed these revelations, Peter came to her and knelt on the floor beside her chair.

His hands, those long, elegant hands she had dreamed of for so many lonely years, reached for the tiny ebony buttons that marched up the front of her habit. He began to unfasten them, beginning with the one on the high collar. He paused at each button, as if to give her time to utter a protest, to stop him.

She did not protest.

He peeled back the close-fitting bodice and the thin silk of her chemise, to reveal the pink, puckered scar at her shoulder. The jagged mark of Chauvin's bullet.

Then, as she held her breath, he leaned forward and touched the scar with his warm, healing mouth.

Carmen cried then, hot tears that fell unchecked down her cheeks, dripping from her chin onto his bent head like a new baptism of truth. She placed her hands on his shoulders, felt their tremble beneath the wool of his jacket. And she felt love, love she had thought gone from her life forever.

"I am so sorry, Carmen," he said, his voice echoing against her skin. He leaned his cheek against her bare shoulder. "So very, very sorry. I can never say that to you enough."

"Peter," she murmured. "*Querido*. If only you knew how many things I must tell you . . ."

The library door opened, Elizabeth and Nicholas

standing on the threshold. They gaped at the tableau before them, Carmen half dressed, Peter kneeling before her with his face pressed to her bosom.

Carmen was so frozen she could not even pull her bodice closed. She could only gape at them in return.

She saw Elizabeth's face, grinning in delight, in the instant before they shut the door and left.

Soon after Carmen's ignominious departure from Clifton House, with her bodice buttoned crookedly and her cheeks stained with tears, Peter himself left the house. He meant to pay a very important call indeed.

On Robert Means.

When Robert opened the door to his lodgings, Peter wasted no time on preliminaries. He grabbed Robert by his shirtfront and shoved him back against the wall. Robert's booted feet dangled from the floor, and he flailed helplessly against Peter's iron grasp.

Robert was a strong man, from all the riding and walking he did in the country. But Peter had always been stronger, and now he had the fire of his fury behind him. He did not even notice the effort it took to keep Robert pinned against the wall.

"Wh-what is this, Clifton?" Robert gasped. His voice was rather faint, due to the fact that his shirtfront was pressed to his larynx.

"I have come to defend a lady's honor," Peter replied calmly. "Surely you have been expecting this."

"What lady?"

"Why, how many ladies have you so defamed? How many ladies have you spread vile falsehoods about?" Peter pressed harder, until Robert's face went quite purple. "Or have you lost count?"

"No, Clifton! I . . ."

"I refer, of course, to only one lady. My wife."

"Your *wife*? Carmen?"

"Just so." Peter released Robert, and watched as he fell into a heap on the floor, gasping. "I demand satisfaction."

Robert stared up at him. He struggled to his feet, but was careful to stay a goodly distance from Peter. "You are challenging me to a duel?"

"Did you, or did you not, tell me the lie that Carmen was Chauvin's lover and a French spy?"

Robert turned away. "I—I suppose I did. But I did not know it was a lie!"

"Then, I have no choice. Name your seconds."

Robert slid back down the wall to a seated position, his face hidden in his hands. His shoulders shook, and Peter suspected he was crying. Or shamming it.

That was a bit discomposing. What was a gentleman supposed to do when the man he had just challenged to a duel burst into tears? Peter was not at all certain, having never fought a duel before.

He reached for a straight-backed chair, swung it about, and straddled it, crossing his arms across the top. "Oh, for pity's sake, don't cry, Robert." He tossed him a handkerchief.

Robert wiped at his face and looked up, still not meeting Peter's gaze. "I never meant for it to be like this. I thought her dead."

"Oh, so it is quite all right to sully a *dead* woman's reputation?"

"No! It—I don't know what came over me that night."

"Do you not?"

"I—perhaps I do. I hated you for having her love. I wanted to hurt you."

Peter shook his head sadly. "And so you did. You ruined my life for six long years. Hers, as well."

"I never meant to hurt Carmen! I loved her. I thought she was dead—beyond pain."

"Well, now you know differently."

Robert began to cry again, sniffling into the handkerchief. "Are you going to shoot me?"

"Do you want me to?"

"Yes, please."

Despite all his pain and anger, Peter could not help but be a bit sorry for such a pitiful, jealousy-consumed creature. "I have a more effective solution."

Robert looked up damply. "What?"

"You will write a letter of apology to Carmen. Then you will leave London, and you will never speak to or of Carmen again. You will never come near any of my family. Do you agree? Or shall I shoot you?"

Robert looked back down again. "I agree. I will leave London, and go back to Cornwall."

"Very well, then. Write that letter, and I shall have it delivered at once. And—have a pleasant journey to Cornwall."

Chapter Eleven

Carmen stood in the doorway of Elizabeth's drawing room at Evanstone Park, and surveyed the crowd assembled there, taking tea, chatting, milling about.

Elizabeth and Nicholas had a very wide acquaintance, and it appeared that they were all gathered for the house party. Attending were Lord and Lady Rivers, an elderly couple who were well-known patrons of the arts. There was a Mrs. King, a very wealthy if somewhat silly widow, who was holding her yapping poodle tightly on her lap, no doubt to prevent it breaking free and biting every ankle in the room.

Elizabeth also included Lord Huntington, a young, handsome viscount, no doubt intended for Carmen. There was a Miss Mary Dixon, an excellent pianist and rather promising artist (Elizabeth was always on the watch for someone to be a mentor to). Miss Dixon was lecturing Lord Crane, a fashionable London beau, on some artistic point, splashing droplets of tea onto his fine green coat with every emphasis.

A vibrant redhead in a bright green silk tea gown held court in one corner, surrounded by laughing gentlemen. No doubt that was Elizabeth's good friend, Mrs. Georgina Beaumont, the famous artist.

And there was Lady Deidra Clearbridge and her

mother. They sat somewhat apart from the noisy fray, their lips slightly pursed.

Only Robert Means was nowhere to be seen. So he had kept the promises in his tearstained letter.

Carmen nodded politely at the Clearbridge ladies as she handed her muff and gloves to the butler. Then her smile widened as she saw Elizabeth hurrying toward her, tugging the redheaded woman along with her.

"My dear Carmen!" Elizabeth cried, kissing her on both cheeks. "You are here at last! You are quite the last to arrive, aside from my naughty brother."

"I do apologize, Lizzie. I had a very late start from Town."

"Well, you are here now, and that is all that matters. Now, you must meet my bosom bow, Mrs. Georgina Beaumont. I lived at her house in Italy before Nicholas and I were married."

"Of course! I have heard so much of the famous Mrs. Beaumont." Carmen turned her smile to the redhead.

Georgina laughed merrily. "Every bit of it true, I assure you!"

Elizabeth grinned. "Georgie quite prides herself on causing a stir everywhere she goes."

"Then, I can see why you are such good friends," Carmen said. "You have such a lot in common."

"*Touché!* But then, we are three of a kind, are we not? You yourself are always the center of attention."

Carmen laughed. "Perhaps you are right, Lizzie."

"I *am* right! What a dash the three of us will cut, now we are all together. But now you must come and have some tea." Elizabeth tucked one of her arms through Carmen's and one through Georgina's, and led them into the drawing room. "You must be parched after your journey. And then you must meet the Richardsons. Such charming people, so fond of art . . ."

Carmen, meant to be choosing a gown for supper, had instead been standing in front of her wardrobe for a full twenty minutes, dressed only in her chemise. She did not see any of the glittering array of garments hanging before her. She ran her hand absently over the skirt of a blue velvet gown, and thought how very much it looked like the blue of Peter's eyes.

She wondered if he would sit next to her at supper . . .

She snatched her hand back from the velvet as if burned. These were the very sort of soppy thoughts she had been trying *not* to have for days now.

The rogue had not called on her after their scene in his library. He had not even sent a note.

Had he forgotten about her the moment she fled his house in embarrassment? *She* had thought of nothing but him ever since that day. Her Ice Earl, her dashing English major. The man who had, once upon a time, held her, loved her, given her a daughter . . .

Isabella!

Carmen slammed the door of the wardrobe, and leaned her forehead against it. In all the tumult of the last few emotional days, she had forgotten the most perplexing problem of all. That Peter had a child he knew nothing about.

She had seen how very angry Peter could be when he felt he had been deceived.

"What to do, what to do?" she muttered, sinking down onto the bed.

"Carmen? Are you in there?" Elizabeth swept into the room without bothering to knock. She was already dressed for the evening, and was pulling on her silk gloves. "We must hurry, or we shall be quite late, and I faithfully promised Nicholas I would not leave him alone with the Riverses. Such bores, the pair of them, but such great ones for commissioning portraits of themselves. I did say that . . ." Then she looked up. "Why, Carmen! You are not even dressed. Where is the maid I sent up to you?"

"I sent her away," Carmen answered quietly.

"Was she unsatisfactory?"

"Not at all. I simply don't think I shall go down tonight, if you will forgive me. I am very tired after the journey."

Elizabeth sat down beside her, with a sigh. "It is my great lout of a brother, is it not? Did he not call after that little—tableau in the library?"

"That was not as it appeared!"

"Um-hm. I'm sure. Well, after you, er, left, he went straight out, and we never saw him again before we left for the country."

"Then, he is not here?" Carmen asked hopefully.

"Oh, he is here. He appeared only an hour ago, with not a word of apology for his lateness."

"Oh."

Elizabeth seized Carmen's hand and pulled her to her feet. "And you must come to dinner! Everyone knows I have the famous condesa here, and they will be quite put out if they do not catch a glimpse of you. My party shall be ruined."

Carmen smiled at that blatant piece of exaggeration. "Well, never have it be said I ruined a party."

"Excellent! And do not worry—I have seated you far from Peter, next to that very nice Viscount Huntington. So Peter can stew in his own envy. Now, what shall you wear?" Elizabeth opened up the wardrobe and began sorting through the gowns.

"I had thought the blue velvet."

"It is pretty, but if Peter is to stew, you need something more—dashing." Elizabeth pulled out a pale gold satin. Carmen had never worn it; it had been purchased for a masked ball in Paris, but she had not been brave enough to wear it when it came to the day. It was cut high at the collarbone, but fluidly followed the lines of the figure.

"This one," said Elizabeth. "Most assuredly."

"Lizzie!" Carmen protested with a laugh. "If I wear that tonight, I will catch my death of cold."

"Not at all! I have plenty of fires lit. And it will make Peter very sorry he did not call."

Carmen giggled.

Peter stood beside the fireplace, and surveyed the crowd gathered in his sister's drawing room before supper.

He might as well have stayed in Town for all the difference it made. Here were so many of the same people he saw there, clustered in the same cliques, repeating the same gossip. Nicholas and a group of gentlemen were having a discussion about some horses that were up for sale in the neighborhood, which would usually have interested Peter at least moderately. But he had wandered away from them after five minutes.

Elizabeth's friend, the famous and dashing artist Mrs. Georgina Beaumont, was at the center of a more daring group, which was talking and laughing loudly, having already dipped into the port and brandy usually saved for after supper. Peter would have liked to join them, if only for the brandy, but they would hardly have welcomed him.

Lady Deidra was seated prettily upon a brocade settee with her mother, her pale pink skirts spread about her like rose petals. She had sent him several glances, but he had no desire to converse with her, either.

All he wanted was to see Carmen.

Then his sister the hostess at last entered her own party. He couldn't help but laugh at how she augmented her meager height with a new headdress of tall crimson plumes that accented her red and gold gown.

Then behind her appeared the very woman he had been longing to see.

She was, as always, in the first stare of fashion, her old trousers and men's shirts obviously left far behind her. Her golden gown modestly covered her collarbone and upper arms, but the fabric was as flowing and shimmering as liquid gold leaf, and followed the lines of her figure and her long legs.

Those long legs that had once wrapped about his own so perfectly . . .

He cursed softly and wished he had some of that brandy.

Then he cursed again, as Carmen turned, and it seemed that Peter—and the entire room—was gazing at her backside in the closely flowing gold satin.

He had such an urge to throw his own coat over her.

He moved behind her so quietly that she did not notice him, and he leaned forward to murmur in her ear.

"Good evening, Condesa," he murmured. His breath lightly stirred the curls at the nape of her neck.

The gold threads of the satin shimmered as she trembled.

But when she turned to face him, her features were perfectly composed, her faintly mocking smile in place. "Good evening, Lord Clifton. I do hope Elizabeth and I have not kept everyone waiting for their supper too long."

"My sister always keeps us waiting. It is her artist's prerogative." He smiled at her, and hoped it looked less like a lupine stretching of lips over teeth than it felt. He longed to be alone with her so very much that it was becoming difficult to display social politeness. "May I escort you in to supper?"

Elizabeth put her hand on her brother's arm. "Now, Peter, you know that is not the way! I have Carmen seated next to that handsome Viscount Huntington, and here he is now to escort her. Would you offer Lady Deidra your arm?" She went up on tiptoe to whisper in his ear. "I did invite her just for you, you know."

All Peter could do was watch helplessly as Carmen moved away from him on Huntington's arm, her soft laughter floating back to him, as if in some enticing dream.

Supper was interminable.

Carmen toyed with her roast duckling, nibbled at the apple compote, and drank more wine than was perhaps strictly prudent. She smiled and chatted with Viscount Huntington, who was most attentive and rather attractive, interested in her travels and her plans for the Season. She may even have flirted with him just the tiniest bit.

But her attention strayed often down the length of the flower-laden table, to where Peter sat between Lady Deidra and her orange satin–clad mother. Deidra spoke with him, quietly, earnestly, her bright head bent near his shoulder. Though he smiled and nodded at her words, Carmen couldn't help but notice that he, too, reached for his wineglass often. He seemed distant from all the merriment and chatter that flowed around them, preoccupied, but always unfailingly polite.

She wished she could read him, so cool and polite, so distant. She wished she could tell what he was thinking; most of all, what he was thinking of *her*. She wanted to tell him all about Isabella, the beautiful, delightful girl they had created together.

If only she could be certain . . .

Carmen sighed and took another sip of her wine.

". . . Would you, Condesa?"

Viscount Huntington's voice drew her back from her imaginings, into the gaiety of the supper table. She blinked up at him.

"I am sorry, Lord Huntington. I must have been woolgathering. Did you ask me something?"

He nodded understandingly. "Quite understandable, I'm sure. The trip from London is quite tiring. I just hope that you are not too tired for the charades after supper."

Carmen was appalled. "Ch-charades?"

"Yes. Lady Elizabeth was just saying that she planned for everyone to draw names for charade teams after supper. We will perform them on Sunday evening."

Now Carmen knew why she had truly never come to England before. It had not been grief. It had been the British propensity for party games. She had hoped to be safe at least at Elizabeth's house! "Well—no, of course not. One can never be too tired for charades."

"Excellent!" He smiled at her shyly. "I hope we are on the same team, Condesa."

She smiled at him, and took another sip of wine. Her gaze slid once again down the table, expecting to find Peter still conversing with Lady Deidra.

Yet Deidra had turned her attention to the gentleman on her left. And Peter was instead watching her, his eyes a warm turquoise in the candlelight. He raised his glass, and in a small, subtle gesture, tilted it in a salute.

Carmen almost choked on her wine.

*   *   *

After the ladies departed to take tea in the drawing room, Peter stayed at the supper table with the other men to sip his port and smoke his cigar. He even managed to engage in the discussion concerning politics and horses with a bit of coherence.

Yet his mind, as always of late, was elsewhere. It was in the drawing room, to be precise, with his wife and her damnably dashing gown!

She was hiding something, he thought. The Carmen he had known in Spain had been more than free with her views and opinions; she had argued with him heatedly on many topics, from politics to art and music, and had never hedged. He thought that it must have arisen from her careful, traditional upbringing; they had been tamped down inside for so long, just waiting to spring free. And he had adored that about her.

This new condesa had certainly learned subtlety. Age had lent her a new beauty and a new careful sophistication.

But she would not meet his gaze directly, would not smile at him with her old, open, sunny ways. Even after their revelations in his library.

What could it be she kept inside her? He burned to know, to understand this new Carmen.

No woman but Carmen, either before or after her, had ever stirred this wild need to *know*, to possess every secret and desire of her heart. After so many years of a frozen anger, his own heart had dared to begin to hope again. There were many things between them, good and terrible, but she still spoke to his soul as no one else ever could.

Yet she still held herself apart!

Could it be she had no feelings left for him, that he had killed them and there was not an ember left in her heart?

Could it be she cared for another? She was so beautiful, so unique. Many men surely desired her.

Men like—that Viscount Huntington Elizabeth had insisted on pairing Carmen with.

Peter looked at the man who was talking with Nicholas. He was a handsome man, Huntington, a wealthy man, so Peter had heard, who lived a quiet, content life in the country. He had been in Spain, as well, but had seemingly left the war behind the instant he returned to England, and had never lost his sweet ways.

Unlike Peter, the darkness had not swallowed him.

Huntington had smiled and talked with Carmen throughout supper, his face open and warm and a bit shy as he watched her. And she had laughed with him, the rich, brandy-dark laughter that Peter had not heard since their wedding night.

Damn Huntington.

Peter tossed back the last of his port and reached for the decanter.

"Well," Nicholas said, too cheerfully in Peter's opinion, as he rose from his chair. "Shall we rejoin the ladies, then? I think Elizabeth was planning some amusement."

"May I join you?"

Carmen looked up from her book, surprised, nay *shocked*, to see Lady Deidra Clearbridge standing beside her chair. The other woman's serene smile was in place, her blue-blue eyes placid, giving no clue as to her motivation in seeking out Carmen. She looked very pleasant, and bland, and English.

What a perfect Countess of Clifton she would make, Carmen reflected wryly.

She smiled in return and tucked away her book. "Of course, Lady Deidra. Please do."

As Deidra sat, her pale pink skirts fluttered about

her like the petals of a dainty rose. She even smelled roselike, and a wreath of white roses twined in her red-gold curls.

Carmen had thought she had long ago left behind her awkward schoolgirl days, towering like a gawky giant over all the other girls at the convent. Now those days came back upon her in a rush.

"I do hope you are enjoying your stay in *our* country, Condesa," Deidra said, her eyes wide and polite over the edge of the teacup she raised to her lips.

"Oh, yes," Carmen answered. "I have found it very charming."

"Though I am certain it cannot be as exciting as Paris, or Italy. Or Spain." One dainty brow rose. "I myself have never wanted to venture away from England. But I did hear you were lately in Paris?"

"Indeed. And before that in Italy, and in Vienna."

"Yes. The Continent is growing ever smaller, is it not? Travel is so very much easier since the end of the war. You must have found it so yourself, being so very well traveled."

"Oh, yes," said Carmen, a bit puzzled. "I have enjoyed great ease of travel. And the variety of company I have encountered is always a pleasure."

The drawing room doors opened then, to admit the gentlemen who had concluded their rituals of port and cigars. Deidra glanced at them briefly before turning her smile back to Carmen. "I presume then that we must soon lose your delightful company to the lure of travel and variety. What a great loss to England."

Carmen eyed her companion impassively, thinking, *Why, the little baggage!* She almost laughed aloud at these attempts to be rid of the foreign interloper. "That is very kind of you to say, Lady Deidra."

"Well, I am very happy, Condesa, that we had this

chance to chat. I am certain we shall see each other
again, before the weekend is concluded."

"I am sure we shall."

Deidra nodded and rose to cross the room in her
graceful pink flutter. She took Peter's arm with her
small hand, and stood on tiptoe to speak quietly in
his ear.

Carmen looked away, into the flames that leapt
high in the marble grate. She could feel a headache
forming behind her eyes, a sharp pain born of confusion, exhaustion, even apprehension. She was just
gathering her book and shawl, to make her excuses
to Elizabeth and then retire, when she felt a warm,
masculine hand alight briefly on her shoulder.

She turned, almost hopeful, to see Viscount Huntington standing behind her. Peter was still across
the room, with Lady Deidra.

Carmen forced herself to smile in welcome, and
patted the arm of the chair that had been recently
vacated by Lady Deidra. Huntington, after all, was a
very amiable gentleman.

He sat down shyly. "I saw that you were conversing with the Clearbridge Pearl, Condesa."

"Is that what she is called? I found her more of
a . . ." Carmen paused. "Rose."

"Oh, yes. That, too. She is much admired. Young
fops compose odes to her eyelashes, that sort of
thing. They say she has had twenty offers."

Carmen laughed. "Was one of them yours, Lord
Huntington?"

He looked affronted. "Lud, no. I couldn't tolerate
being leg-shackled to such alabaster dignity my
whole life, even if she would accept my addresses.
Pardon my saying so, Condesa."

"Of course. But why would she not accept your
addresses? You seem a very nice young man to me."

He blushed a bright pink, all the way into his cravat. "I'm not top-lofty enough for an earl's daughter!"

"Ah."

Then Elizabeth interrupted their conversation, swooping down upon them with folded bits of paper clutched in her hand.

"Oh, Carmen, there you are!" she cried. "Do forgive me, Huntington, for stealing her away, but I simply must beg her assistance in setting up my game."

"Elizabeth," Carmen protested, "if it is charades, I do not know how . . ."

"Not at all! I would not have *charades* at my party. This is *tableaux*."

Carmen did not see how that was any different. "Tableaux?"

"Yes. Here, hold these papers for me." Elizabeth had gathered a crowd with her enthusiasm, and she now clambered onto a chair to make her instructions heard. "Every team will be assigned a scene from Greek mythology to enact. The team which is the most dramatic, the most convincing, shall win the prize!" A small murmur of excitement arose, and she raised her hand for silence. She flashed a brilliant smile at Carmen, and then turned one onto her brother. "I shall assign the first scene to none other than my own brother, Lord Clifton, who, along with the Condesa de Santiago, shall enact Endymion and Selene!"

Carmen closed her eyes. She could hear Lady Deidra's hissing whisper, "Well, this is a most shocking pastime! I must say I had hoped Lady Elizabeth would show more propriety, despite being an *artist*."

Yet, even with her eyes squeezed shut and her ears trying to do so, Carmen could feel the weight of Peter's regard from across the room as he watched her. When she opened her eyes to look back at him, to beseech him to talk some sense into his sister, he *winked* at her!

"Psst! Carmen! Are you awake?"

Carmen rolled over in her bed and blinked sleepily, certain she must be dreaming. But when she pinched herself, it did not go away. Elizabeth still stood at her bedside, wrapped in a cloak, a lantern held aloft.

"I am now," Carmen said, sitting up and rubbing her eyes. "Whatever are you about, Lizzie?"

"Some of us are going out to look at the moon from the medieval ruins nearby. It is full tonight, you know. So romantic!"

"The ruins? But it must be after midnight!"

"Nearly two, I believe. Do you want to come?"

Carmen glanced at her window, at the bar of silvery moonlight that spilled from between the velvet drapes. She could feel the old excitement of adventure tingling in her fingertips again, something that had not happened for so very long.

The fact that this adventure was looking at the moon at two in the morning rather than facing French guns made it all the better.

"I may as well, since I am already awake." She climbed out of the bed and reached into the wardrobe for a plain muslin day dress and her cloak.

The others were already waiting for them on the drive. There was Georgina Beaumont, who carried a large picnic hamper; Nicholas, with a bottle of champagne; Lord Huntington, and Miss Dixon. And Peter.

Lady Deidra and her mother were nowhere in sight.

Elizabeth and Nicholas led the way down a narrow, tree-lined pathway that veered off of the main drive, closely followed by the chattering, laughing group. Carmen and Peter brought up the rear.

"I saw that Robert Means declined Elizabeth's invitation," she said quietly.

"Yes. I do believe that he has kept his word to me, and retired to the country for good. I went to see him after—well, after we spoke in my library. He promised he would leave London." Peter's hand sought hers, warm and reassuring in the chilly darkness. "He will not be bothering you again."

Carmen squeezed his hand. "He never *bothered* me. That is what makes his lies so very shocking."

"Perhaps even more shocking than that I would believe them?"

"Perhaps," Carmen whispered.

Peter jumped lightly over a fallen log, and reached back to assist Carmen, swinging her up into his arms.

When she was on the other side of the log, he did not release her, but held her against him. Carmen looped her arms about his neck and looked down at his lovely, patrician face, illuminated by moonlight.

"I can never say I am sorry enough, Carmen," he said softly. "I should have had more faith in you, in our feelings for one another."

"So you should have," she answered lightly. "But I have already forgiven you."

"Come along, you two!" called Elizabeth. "No lagging behind, if you please. What kind of chaperone do you think I am? Even if I *am* an artist!"

The others shrieked with laughter.

Peter placed Carmen on her feet and wordlessly offered his arm. She took it, and they walked together into the clearing where the medieval watch tower, half ruined, stood sentinel.

Some of the others were already climbing up inside the tower, and their laughter cast a warm golden glow over the ancient stones. A stream rushed along behind it, its gurgle and tumble mingling with that laughter.

The moon bathed the whole scene in a gentle, silvery luminescence, giving it the unreal atmosphere of a painting.

Carmen thought it the perfect setting for a reawakening love.

Georgina leaned out of a window at the very top of the tower, her long red hair falling over her shoulders. "Look!" she called. "I am Rapunzel!"

Carmen laughed as she took in the whole enchanted, fairy-tale scene. "Is it not wonderful?"

"Lovely," Peter said. "It is an enchanted night."

"That is exactly what I thought." Carmen looked up at him, to find he was watching her. "I am so happy we are sharing this together, Peter. I thought never to see such a thing with you again."

"Neither did I, Carmen," he answered. He raised her hand to his lips and pressed a tender, lingering kiss to her wrist. "Neither did I."

Chapter Twelve

"'Endymion the shepherd . . . the moon Selene, saw him, loved him sought him . . . Kissed him, lay beside him.' Hmph."

Carmen tossed aside the volume of Theocritus she was perusing over her morning chocolate. She slid down among the mound of pillows on her bed, and turned her face into the lavender-scented linen with a giggle.

Nothing, not even hiding her face, could erase the persistent vision of Peter clad in nothing but a brief, a *very* brief, chiton. And perhaps a pair of sandals.

She was beginning to suspect that Elizabeth, seemingly so very charming and sweet, was nothing but an imp.

Endymion and Selene, indeed! Carmen shuddered to think of what Elizabeth might conjure up next, in her misguided scheming.

"Carmen?" Elizabeth knocked softly at the door, seemingly conjured by Carmen's thoughts. "Are you awake?"

"No," Carmen called.

Elizabeth came inside anyway, already carefully coiffed and dressed in blue muslin and a lacy shawl. "I so need your assistance in organizing today's excursion!"

Carmen pulled the bedclothes down from over her

head, and peered at Elizabeth over the edge. "Not if it involves bloody tableaux."

"Tsk tsk. Wherever did you learn such language? And the tableaux are our grand finale for Sunday." She paused. "Though today would be an excellent opportunity for rehearsal. I was thinking of a small picnic at the tower we went to last night. The day looks to be a wonderful, sunny one, and you should see the tower in the light!"

"That does sound delightful," Carmen answered reluctantly.

"I knew you would think so! Now, I must tell the others, so that we may be off directly after breakfast." Elizabeth began to turn away, then paused, reaching into her pocket for a small bundle of letters. "I very nearly forgot! These came for you with the morning post."

Carmen took the letters from her, but waited until she was alone again to peruse them. One was from Esperanza, with a carefully penned postscript from Isabella, detailing all they had been doing in Carmen's absence (a pantomime at the Sadler's Wells Theater seemed foremost among them). There were also two missives from friends in Paris, full of lively and amusing gossip.

And the last—the last was written on cheap, smudged paper and sealed with black wax.

Carmen dropped the letter, one hand pressed to her mouth to stifle a cry. How could they have found her. How could they have known where she was?

They were everywhere now. She was safe nowhere.

"I believe I owe you an apology, Carmen."

Carmen, who had deliberately wandered from the others on their picnic excursion in order to be quiet and think, whirled around with a gasp at the unexpected sound of Peter's voice. She crumpled the letter in her hand, pressing it tightly against the folds of her skirt.

He stood at the edge of the small circle of trees Carmen had found beside the stream, poised hesitantly, as if unsure of his welcome and prepared to instantly depart.

He was so achingly handsome, with the sunlight falling across his windswept golden hair, gilding it like a Greek icon. Carmen could almost have wept at his loveliness.

"Another apology?" she said. "What have you done this time?"

"For Lizzie's—overly eager behavior. She has the artistic temperament, you know, and once she has a goal in mind she will not relinquish it." He paused, watching the stream just beyond her figure. "I had the impression that she made you uncomfortable with her silly tableaux, which she no doubt learned about in Italy, and I wanted to be certain you knew you were under no obligation to go along with her. I could speak with her."

"Oh, no," Carmen protested. "I would not like to ruin Lizzie's plans. Unless, that is, *you* do not wish to participate in the tableaux." She glanced at him to gauge his reaction, but his expression was only very polite.

Then he smiled, the odd, crooked half smile that always made her stomach leap into her throat with no warning at all. "And forfeit the sight of you in a chiton, Carmen? Certainly not."

"How very strange."

"Strange? That a man should want to see you in a chiton?"

Carmen laughed, her mood instantly lightened. "I should hope not! Only odd because I had thought exactly the same about you. But I added sandals to the ensemble."

Peter's eyes widened, and Carmen feared she had ventured too far into flirting. It was early days yet, after all. She turned away to look at the water. "Is it not lovely here? So very peaceful."

"Beautiful." Peter moved to stand behind her, his breath warm on her cheek. "I used to come here often."

"I thought that Elizabeth and Nicholas only recently purchased the property?"

"Oh, yes. But it is only a short ride from here to Clifton Manor. Old Lord Mountebank, the former owner, never cared if we ran wild here as children."

"Clifton Manor. Your home." Peter had spoken to her often of Clifton Manor while they were in Spain. He had told her of the house, of how it began life as a Tudor manor, the long-ago dowry of an Elizabethan bride to the second earl, and of how each earl had added to it until it was a sprawling amalgamation. He had told her of the hidey-holes he and Elizabeth had found as children, of the great gardens, and the lake with its Oriental summerhouse.

She had always felt as if she could see it, touch it, feel its spell woven of so many generations of love and laughter, reaching out to enfold her in its history.

Once, for a brief while, she had thought to be its mistress. To belong there, as Peter and Elizabeth did. To watch her children playing in the gardens.

Then she had known she would never live there.

"Yes," said Peter. "My home."

Carmen sat down on the grassy bank of the stream, tucking the thick green velvet of her habit beneath her against the damp. "Was it still all you had dreamed of when you returned there after Spain?"

He sat beside her, his long legs in their fashionable doeskin breeches stretched out before him. "Clifton had not changed at all. That is the beauty of it. It was still as green and peaceful as ever. It even smelled the same, of wax candles and beeswax polish. But I had changed. So much, too much. That I had not counted on. I had foolishly thought that when I came home I would be the same as before I left. I would forget the war and be at peace."

"Yes," said Carmen with a sigh. "I felt the very same, when I went home to my family's house in Seville. I thought I could rejoin society, be a devout Spanish lady again."

"When did you go back?"

"After I learned that you were dead. I was so exhausted, so ill. I only wanted to go home. Though my parents were long dead, I still thought of that house, so dark and quiet, as home. The places I had known as a child. I, too, thought I could forget and be at peace. So I went back, and I never spoke of what had happened, not to anyone." Her fingers closed tighter about the crumpled letter she still held in her hand. The edges of the paper cut into her palm. "I only discovered, as we all must, that peace is only to be found in my heart. And my peace had gone."

Peter leaned back on his elbows to look up at the sky above them, covered by the interlocking branches of the tress. The laughter of the group could be heard faintly as they climbed up inside the tower. The two of them seemed enclosed in a world of their own, though.

"Did Elizabeth tell you how I was ill when I returned home?" Peter said.

Carmen looked down at him, at his beautiful, still face. "Nicholas said that it was difficult for you. That you were not at all yourself. Did you have a fever from your wounds?"

"I was ill in my mind. I could not forget you, never leave what had happened between us behind me. It made me cruel, especially to my poor sister. All I could ever think about, ever see, was you."

"Yes," she whispered. "And I you."

He touched her then, his hand warm on her arm, burning through the heavy fabric of her sleeve. She leaned against him and closed her eyes, letting herself feel, just for the moment, a measure of the security she had longed for for so long.

"This place," Peter said. "Does it not remind you of another we have seen?"

She smiled without opening her eyes. "That river in Spain, near your camp. Where you asked me to dance . . ."

"And asked you to be my wife."

"And I said yes, yes, yes!"

"And where I kissed you . . ."

Carmen laughed. "I do believe we did much more than kiss!"

Peter laughed, too, a rich sound rusty from disuse. "Oh, yes! I also recall that."

Carmen opened her eyes and smiled at him. How could anyone call him the *Ice* Earl, she mused, when he was as golden and alive as the sun.

He gently reached up and touched her face, cradling her cheek in his palm as if it were the most precious, fragile crystal. "Carmen. Are you truly here with me, alive, or are you another dream?"

"I could ask the same of you," she murmured. "I dreamed of a moment like this one so often during these years. Am I awake? Is this real?"

"Does this feel real to you?" Peter sat up and touched his lips softly to hers.

It was so strange, so familiar, so thrilling. Carmen leaned closer into the kiss, opening her lips under his inquisitive pressure. Her fingers reached to touch the satin of his hair, to feel him against her . . .

"Lord Clifton? Are you here?"

"I say, Clifton? Are you hiding from us?"

Carmen gasped at the sound of voices—Lady Deidra and Viscount Huntington. She pulled her mouth from Peter's, drew out of his reaching arms to scramble to her feet. She brushed at her skirts, frantically trying to disentangle leaves and grass from the velvet.

It was a hopeless cause. She simply looked too much like a woman who had been rolling about on the ground, right to the guilty flush she was sure must be staining her cheeks.

"What was I thinking of?" she muttered. "Anyone could have seen us! What a scandal! What if . . ."

Peter also rose to his feet, somewhat stiffly, and attempted to come to her aid. "Carmen, I never . . ."

He held out his hand to her, but she did not see it, stumbling back out of the clearing.

"Oh, Peter!" she cried. "Do not say you are sorry again! I couldn't bear it."

"Then please, let me . . ."

She turned away from him and scooped up her hat and gloves from where they lay on the ground. "I must be alone right now, must—think. But we will speak later, Peter, I promise. It is only that—oh, it is *nothing*!"

Then she rushed away to where the others were gathered beside the tower, brushing past Huntington and Deidra with only a distracted nod.

She did not even notice the balled-up, smeared note that had fallen from her hand, only to be found by a very puzzled Peter.

His face darkened as he read it, a rushing fury thundering in his ears. "By damn," he whispered.

"Lord Clifton?" Deidra asked softly. "Is something amiss?"

He forced himself to look up at her serene face,

and smiled tightly. "Not at all. Lady Deidra. Not at all."

"I do not understand women in the least!"

Elizabeth looked up from the menus she was perusing to blink at her brother in surprise. He very seldom came into her personal rooms at all, let alone unannounced, to throw himself into a chair and make odd pronouncements.

"You, Peter? Not understand women?" she said with a snort. "I can scarce fathom that. They are always flocking about you so."

"That does not mean I understand them; quite the opposite. The more I meet, the less I understand. And why should women want to *flock* at all?" He leaned his head back against the satin cushions of the chair, and closed his eyes. Yet he could still see Carmen by the stream, her dark hair tousled, her lips red from his kiss. The image seemed emblazoned on his eyelids, there for all time. "And Carmen de Santiago is the worst of the lot."

"Ah, yes." Elizabeth nodded sagely. "I often said the very same when I first met Nick—men are unfathomable, and Nicholas Hollingsworth is the very worst. I still think that, on occasion. That is what love does to a person, I suppose."

"Love!"

"Yes. You love Carmen. There is no use in denying it."

Peter could feel a blinding headache coming upon him, born of having to deal with *females*, whether they were mercurial wives-who-weren't-wives, or too wise sisters. He shook his head slowly. "I was not going to deny it. I do love her. I have since I first saw her, and I suppose I never truly stopped. Even when she was dead."

"Then, what is wrong?"

"I do not know!" Peter slapped his open palm against the arm of the chair. "It is Carmen. Every time it seems we may become close again, every time I try to understand her, she shies away like a skittish colt. She runs from me." He remembered Carmen in Spain, on that afternoon by the river. How she would spin away from his arms, laughing, beckoning, her long curtain of hair spilling about her. It seemed she was still doing that. "She was always elusive as water, so intent on her independence. She always said she would never be as helpless as she was with her dreadful first husband again. Perhaps it is only the same thing now."

"Hm. Perhaps."

"But she knows I am not him! And somehow it seems—different now. She seems rather desperate, in some way."

"Well, she *is* Spanish. You can hardly expect her to be a predictable little English rose, like Lady Deidra. She has had a very difficult time these last years, just as you have. She is not one to trust easily, especially in the appearance of happy times at last. You know what that is like, brother, because you are just the same." Elizabeth tapped her fingertips thoughtfully against her desk. "Perhaps your only real difficulty lies in a lack of communication. Perhaps Carmen thinks that you still mean to marry Lady Deidra, and that you are just trifling with her emotions."

Peter snorted. "How absurd! How can I possibly marry someone like Lady Deidra when Carmen is alive? There is no other woman for me in the world but her."

"Yes, but does Carmen know that? You were not very kind to her when she first appeared in London. You made it obvious that you had made a new life without her, that you had nothing but contempt for her."

"I never felt contempt," Peter protested. "I was only—confused. But that is all changed now! *Everything* has changed since she came back into my life. I felt frozen before, but now . . ." His voice fell away, unable to give words to his tumult of emotions. He held out his hands helplessly. "It has all changed because of her."

"I know that, Peter," said Elizabeth. "Does Carmen, though? She is as lost and confused as you are."

"Then, what can I do?"

"Talk to her, of course, you nodcock! Go to her, and tell her everything you have just told me. Hold nothing back. And, in exchange, you may hear some pleasant surprises of your own."

She held out her hand to him, and he clasped it tightly.

"Can I do that?" he murmured half to himself.

"You *must*. My brother, I know how you love to keep your own counsel, hide your emotions, but you must not do that now. Not if you want your wife, value your family. Do not be foolish, as I so very nearly was with my Nicholas."

"Of course you are right, as always." Peter stood and kissed his sister's cheek. "How did you ever become so wise, little Lizzie?"

"Oh, I have learned a great deal from the travails of marriage! As, I hope, have you."

"Marriage is indeed a travail. But I will do as you say, and go speak with Carmen now. We have a great deal to discuss." He reached into his coat pocket and touched the crumpled letter Carmen had lost. "A very great deal."

Elizabeth gave a small laugh. "Oh, Peter. If only you knew." She looked back to her menus, but then called after him. "If you need an excuse to go to her chamber, just say I sent you to rehearse for the tableaux!"

Chapter Thirteen

Carmen stared down into her trunk, at the jumble of gowns and underpinnings she had just tossed in. She hardly knew what she was doing, or why; she only had a desperate need to leave, to go to her daughter and hold her in her arms again, and know that she was safe.

Carmen leaned her forehead against the edge of the trunk lid, suddenly dizzy. What was *wrong* with her? Why was she suddenly dashing about like an escapee from Bedlam? Because Peter had kissed her?

It was not as if he had not done a great deal more than *kiss* her in the past!

But such had always been the way when she was with him. She had always considered herself rather levelheaded, yet when she saw him she was not herself, not the cool, sophisticated condesa. She became giddy, giggly, uncertain, wildly ecstatic.

She loved him, that was obvious. That had not, would never, change.

She also loved her daughter and feared more than anything to lose her. It was not at all a rational fear—the chances of Peter snatching her away were slim indeed. But there it was. Isabella had been an enormous, unasked for gift at a time in Carmen's life when she had seen nothing but fear and grief. Isabella had been her joy and her light for six years, and something in the back of Carmen's heart feared that light could be snatched away as suddenly as it had been bestowed.

She knew, of course, that Peter would have to be told of his child. She just did not know how.

A knock sounded at the door. Carmen, thinking it must be Elizabeth come to see how she was after her swift departure from their picnic, straightened and wiped at her damp cheeks. "Come in!"

It was not Elizabeth. It was Peter, utterly composed, unearthly handsome. Almost as if the untidy scene beside the stream had never occurred.

Then she looked into his eyes and saw that they were no longer ice blue, but a stormy gray.

As she just stared at him, unable to make her throat work to say a word, he stepped into the room and closed the door behind him.

"I . . ." he began, then stopped. His gaze dropped from hers, moved around the room restlessly.

The Ice Earl at a loss for words? Impossible! Carmen closed the lid of the trunk and sat down upon it, to await what he had come to say.

"Lizzy told me to say I have come to rehearse for the tableaux," he said at last.

Carmen laughed, all her fright and tension melting away at his absurdity. "Oh, Peter! Then, where is your tunic? No, you cannot fool me."

"No. Of course I did not come to discuss my sister's silly party games." He leaned back against the door, his eyes still wary as he watched her. "I wanted to say that if I did or said anything to offend you, then I am deeply sorry."

"We are a strange pair, Peter," she sighed. "After all we have been to each other, we should be beyond so very many apologies."

"So we should. But things are rather—complicated between us. I should not have rushed at you in that manner." He grinned at her halfheartedly. "You were always as changeable as the wind."

She smiled in return. "As were you. My unpredictable, dashing English major. It was why I married you."

"My unpredictability? And here I thought it was for my dashing regimentals."

"Because you understood me, as no one else, not even my parents, ever could! You never attempted to change me, to make me more ladylike or something." Carmen pleated the fabric of her skirt restlessly between her fingers, lost for a moment in memories of those heady days of first love. She looked up suddenly and saw from the rare softness on Peter's face that he, too, was thinking of the same things.

"I am sorry," she said, "that I dashed away from you this morning. I am tired, I suppose. I have been a bit, well, unsteady of late."

"I think I know why that may be, Carmen."

"Do you, indeed? As I said, you always were able to know me better than anyone else, but . . ."

He silently held out the letter she had lost beside the stream, now hopelessly crumpled and soiled.

Carmen bit her lip. Peter was the very last person she would want to know of her troubles! He knew all about that time in her life; he carried the darkness of the same time in his own heart. He had even suspected her of the same things the letter writer spoke of.

Could still suspect her, perhaps?

In the midst of her dismay, the thought flitted through her mind that perhaps *Peter* had written the letters. She dismissed that thought immediately. Not only had his shock on the night of the Dacey ball been very real, but she knew Peter as well as he knew her. If he believed that she had done those things, he would not have written foul, anonymous letters.

He would have faced her directly and shot her in the heart.

Carmen forced back the insistent urge to flee, and forced herself to remain where she was, seated on the closed trunk. She folded her hands carefully in her lap.

"Now you know why I came to England," she said softly.

"Do you mean to say that you were receiving these—these *things* even abroad?"

"Of course. Four of them in Paris, two here. I traced the ones I received in France to England, and I knew that I would have to come here if I was to find the culprit. I meant to track down every person I had met during the war, and hound them until I found the right one." Her gaze fell to her clasped hands, to the emerald that glowed on her finger. "Otherwise I would never have come to England."

"Why? Do you hate it here so very much?"

Carmen laughed, more a small hiccup than a true laugh. "Peter, what a true Englishman you are! I do not hate England. It is all these English voices. It was hard enough to hear them in France or Italy. I would hear an Englishman speaking behind me on the street sometimes, and I would turn, so full of hope, thinking it would be you." She pressed the back of her hand against her eyes, unwilling to look at him as she poured out these embarrassing confessions. "I knew it would be so much worse here, where I would see things and places you had told me about. That we had planned to see together. It would have been—awful."

She heard him move then, the soft rustle of his superfine coat as he came across the room to kneel beside her. His hand was cool as he laid it softly on hers, and she peeked up at him cautiously.

"When I came back from Spain," he said, "I saw you in every black-haired woman, every red flower, like the ones you carried at our wedding. Every emerald. I felt like my soul had been torn to shreds from losing you, and in such a terrible way. I could never have gone back to Spain."

Carmen had never so longed to weep in all her life. "Peter, *querido*," she said. Then she could say no more. She simply placed her other hand atop his, and they sat there in silence for several long, sweet moments.

Then Peter shook his head fiercely, as if clearing it of a dream, and gently drew away from her. He pulled a chair near to her trunk and sat down.

His eyes, so gray with roiling emotions only a moment before, were now ice blue with resolve. Carmen remembered just such a determined look on his face from military meetings during the war.

"You say you received four of these letters in Paris," he said.

Carmen drew in a deep breath. She had to focus on the business at hand now, not the bittersweet might-have-beens of her marriage. "Yes. And two since I came to England. One at my house in Town . . ."

"And one under my sister's very roof," Peter finished, steel in his voice.

"I knew that I would have to find whoever is doing this, and put a final stop to it. Or I will never be left in peace. I have not paid anything."

"Quite right. Do you have any idea at all of the villain's identity? Could it possibly be our friend Robert Means?"

"I had thought of Robert, of course. Especially after you told me of his perfidy. But, despite what he did,

I believe he truly thought me dead. And, if he truly was in Cornwall all this time, it would have taken much longer for me to receive the London letter." She shook her head. "So no, I do not think it is him. But I don't know who else it could be." Then she smiled teasingly. "It is only too bad it was *not* Robert. I could have ferreted him out so very easily, you know. I would simply have worn my most dashing gowns, laughed at all his witticisms, leaned subtly against his arm at supper, pressing my bosom . . ."

Peter seized her around the waist then and pulled her onto his lap, both of them laughing helplessly until tears ran down their faces. "I am glad, then, it was *not* Robert," he gasped, his breath soft on her hair. "If that is what you were planning, madam!"

Carmen leaned her forehead against his chest, still giggling. He smelled wonderful, of soap and clean starch and sunlight. She closed her eyes and tried to inhale him inside of her.

He pulled her even closer to him and pressed his lips against her temple. "We *will* find whoever is doing this, Carmen, and he will pay. I promise you are quite safe now."

"Yes," she murmured. "I cannot say how very many times I have longed to be a *we* again, not fighting the demons all alone."

"You are not alone."

"No." Carmen rested her head on his shoulder and smiled against the fine cloth of his coat. "Not anymore. And neither are you."

There was a rustle in the corridor, a hum of voices and laughter as a group passed her door and went down the staircase. Carmen looked at the window and saw to her surprise that it was full dark out. They would be expected at supper very soon.

She drew away from the warm shelter of Peter's arms and stood up. "We should be dressing for sup-

per," she said. "Elizabeth will wonder what has become of us."

Peter also rose. "Not my sister! She will assume
we are dutifully rehearsing for her dreaded tableaux
and all her matchmaking efforts have been successful. But, yes, I should be going. We must put our
plan of action in motion this evening, and find out
the villain. Perhaps we could speak some more with
Lord Crane. I understand that, despite his peacock
ways, he was in Spain."

Carmen waved her hand airily. "Oh, yes! The plan
of action. Low-cut gowns and bosoms. Do you think
they would have an effect on Lord Crane?"

"Not *that* plan!" Peter took up her hand and
pressed a lingering kiss on her palm. "I am very glad
that you have confided in me, Carmen. Now there
are no more secrets between us. We may begin
afresh."

"Yes," she murmured as she watched him walk
out the door. "No more secrets."

Only the greatest secret of all. His child.

Chapter Fourteen

Carmen sat on Nicholas's left at supper, half listening to him as he spoke of a planned balloon
ascension from Hyde Park that he wanted to escort
her and Elizabeth to when they returned to Town.
She smiled and murmured at all the appropriate
pauses, and even managed to ask pertinent questions
every so often. She partook of the excellent dishes
Elizabeth's new French chef had prepared, and tried
not to partake too freely of the excellent French
wines. Yet even the lobster patties may just as well
have been sawdust.

Too many thoughts swirled in her mind for her to
completely throw herself into the merry party the
Hollingsworths had worked so hard to create. She
was thinking of the cruel blackmailer, that could possibly hide behind a laughing and friendly facade just
like the ones about her. She thought of Peter, and
the tender scene they had shared. She thought of
Elizabeth's announcement that Lady Deidra and her
mother had been called home suddenly, and had left
Evanstone Park. She wondered if that meant a final
severing of Peter's old intentions toward Deidra and
a new commitment toward herself.

She thought of her precious daughter, the daughter
she had to tell Peter about very soon, and if she
dared to hope such a thing.

Surely the man who had held her in his arms and

promised her she was no longer alone was someone
she could trust Isabella with? Or was she being too
hasty, too hopeful?

". . . don't you agree, Condesa?"

Carmen shook off her daze to smile at the woman
seated across from her, who had apparently been
speaking to her. A Mrs. King, if she was not mistaken, a lady who always seemed to favor grandiose
headdresses of fruits and flowers.

"I do beg your pardon," Carmen said. "I fear I
could not hear your question, Mrs. King."

"Oh, yes!" Mrs. King answered gaily. "Lady Elizabeth's parties are always so *loudly* delightful! I was
only speaking of the tableaux planned for Sunday
evening. Such a quiz! Do you not agree?"

"Oh, yes. Indeed. A quiz."

"Nicholas is in my little group." Mrs. King wag-
gled flirtatious fingers at Nicholas. "As are the Richardsons. We are to enact Hermes and Athena coming
to the aid of Perseus and Andromeda." She giggled.
"I am to be Athena! I have found the most delightful
armored breastplate in the attic."

"Ah," Carmen said, not entirely attending. "But
your eyes are brown, Mrs. King."

Mrs. King blinked her brown eyes. "My eyes,
Condesa?"

"Yes. They are not gray." When Mrs. King contin-
ued to look blank, she continued. " 'And gray-eyed
Athena cried, Give the Greeks a bitter homecoming.
Stir up your waters with wild whirlwinds—let dead
men choke the bays and line the shores and reefs.' "
So Theocritus had proved useful after all.

Mrs. King went a trifle pale at the mention of dead
bodies, that could possibly clutter up her tableau.
"Well. Yes, Condesa. But these are *silent* tableaux,
you know. I needn't learn any lines. Need I?"

Carmen took a sip of her wine and smiled reassuringly. "I shouldn't think so. All you need do is look martial in your breastplate."

"Oh, good!" Mrs. King cried in relief. "You are to enact a tableau with Lord Clifton, are you not, Condesa?"

Carmen nodded. "Endymion and Selene."

"Yes. I did hear that that is the true reason Lady Deidra Clearbridge and her mother left." Mrs. King looked down the table at Peter, who was talking with his sister. "He is so very handsome. You are so *fortunate*. How I wish I could have been chosen for his team! If I did not have my dear Mr. King to think of . . ." She giggled.

Carmen was saved from replying by the arrival of dessert. She took a very large spoonful of the lemon trifle.

Ah, yes. Very fortunate indeed.

"We must have dancing!" Elizabeth announced. After supper, when the gentlemen had rejoined the ladies in the drawing room, small groups had begun to break off and drift away to various corners, but her words brought them back.

"Dancing?"

"What fun!"

"Yes," said Elizabeth. "The gentlemen will push back the furniture, so we needn't waste time by having the ballroom opened. Miss Dixon, if you could oblige us with your delightful playing? A country-dance, I think, since we *are* in the country."

As Miss Dixon struck up a lively tune at the pianoforte, Elizabeth took her brother's arm and drew him onto the cleared floor.

Georgina Beaumont and Lord Richardson followed, and soon ten couples had taken their places in the set. The drawing room was a blur of jewel-bright gowns, music, and laughter.

Carmen watched it all from her perch on a settee, laughing as Peter swung Elizabeth about so energetically in the turns that her small feet left the floor and her skirts flew out in a shining sea-green silk arc.

She thought, as she watched all the merriment and calling out that went on, how very much more comfortable a country party was than a London party. It was all good fun among friends. Perhaps, she reflected, a country life with a husband and children would not be such a terrible thing. Especially after the tumult of her travels.

As the country-dance wound to its rowdy finish, Georgina Beaumont clapped her hands and called, "We must now have a waltz!" The dramatic redhead lifted the hem of her purple satin gown and twirled about her partner, to the applause of the others.

Miss Dixon said, "But I have not permission to waltz, Mrs. Beaumont!"

"Pooh!" said Georgina with a laugh. "This is not Almack's, Miss Dixon dear. Lady Jersey will not catch you here. Will she, Lizzie? You do not have any patronesses lurking behind your curtains?"

"No, indeed!" Elizabeth answered. "Everyone is quite safe here. But perhaps you would prefer to continue playing to dancing, Miss Dixon? You played that last dance so beautifully."

With that, she took her husband's arm in one hand and Peter's in the other, and marched them over to Carmen's settee. "Here now, Carmen! Why are you sitting here all alone like such a matron? No one is allowed to be so serious and solitary at my party!"

"I do apologize, Lizzie," Carmen answered with a laugh. "I vow to be nothing but merry and gay for the rest of your weekend."

"That is more the thing," Elizabeth said. "Nick has promised to dance with me, so unfashionable to dance with one's wife, though I suppose we are allowed in our own home! So, Carmen dear, you must dance with Peter. We must not let him feel neglected, must we?''

Then, not giving her a chance to reply, she tugged on her husband's arm and led him onto the floor.

Nicholas grinned at them over his shoulder and shrugged.

Carmen started to plead exhaustion, but then she looked up at Peter's face. He looked positively— could it be *eager*? He was even smiling, without a hint of mockery.

That smile faded a bit as Carmen frowned in puzzlement. "We do not have to dance, you know," he said. "If you are too fatigued."

"Oh, I think we *must* dance, or Lizzie will surely have a fit and come *make* us dance!" She rose to her feet and laid her hand softly on his sleeve. "And I do so love a waltz. Remember?"

His smile returned. "Then, by all means . . ."

He led her onto the floor, just as Miss Dixon struck the opening chords of a Viennese waltz. His shoulder was warm and strong, the muscles tensed beneath the velvet of his coat as she touched him. His hand clasped hers firmly, and they swung into the dance, far closer than propriety allowed.

It was not a sunlit Spanish riverbank this time; Carmen's trousers and boots were now an elegant blue velvet gown, and Peter's regimentals were long gone. Years of pain and experience lay between the people they had been on that day, and the people that they were now.

But somehow that made this moment, this dance, all the more sweet. They had struggled long and hard to reach it, this instant of swaying together in a ballroom, her skirts wrapping about his legs as he twirled her around and around.

As Carmen looked up at Peter, into his sky-blue

eyes, she knew that he felt the same. She knew, without a doubt, that it would be safe to trust him with her most precious possessions, her daughter and her heart. For now, and for all the future to come.

As the music ended, she leaned forward to whisper in his ear.

"I must speak with you, Peter. There are things— many things I must tell you. Will you come to me tonight?"

His warm breath stirred the curls at her temple as he whispered back, "As you wish, Condesa."

Chapter Fifteen

Peter sat alone in his room for a long time after the rest of the household had retired, not lighting candles, just sitting beside the small, flickering fire. He sipped slowly on a snifter of brandy, and listened as a small group of late-goers talked and laughed in the corridor.

At last, in the very darkest part of the night, all was silent. Except for the soft, creeping sounds of people slipping illicitly toward bedrooms not their own.

As he should be doing, though it seemed a bit foolish to be sneaking into his own wife's room. He knew she was waiting for him, waiting to impart whatever dire secrets she was holding. And he fairly ached to go to her, to see her again, even if he had only been parted from her hours ago. He felt like some overeager schoolboy, hungry to hold her in his arms, to smell her perfume.

But he hesitated.

He poured himself another measure of brandy. So many things had changed since he had lost her, his beautiful Carmen, his dashing Spanish bride. He had never in his life before her thought he could love someone so intensely, find the presence of another person in the world to be so vital to his own existence. When he had lost her so horribly, it had been as if all light and beauty had left him forever, and he had known that he could never feel so strongly about a woman again.

So he had thought to contract a loveless, convenient union. Then Carmen had flown back into his life like a sparkling star, and he had seen how impossible such a bloodless life would be. He had known a great love; no convenience could ever compare.

The knowledge of her innocence, of Robert's lies, had freed him of the dreadful weight he had carried for so long, had made him finally cease to look back, to move forward into life.

Forward with her.

When they had danced that night, he had truly laughed, had felt free and light with her in his arms. He had felt truly alive, perhaps for the first time since their wedding night. He loved her; he wanted the life they had dreamed of together, at long last.

All of which made him reluctant to go to her. He took another sip of brandy.

He was not a man who easily trusted deep emotions, unlike his sister, who rushed into them headlong. They so often seemed the herald of disaster. And Carmen's eyes had been so dark and serious when she whispered that there was something she must tell him. Something that could not be kept from him for another night.

Peter was sick to death of secrets. He wanted nothing more than to move into the future fresh and free, and he knew that to do that Carmen must unburden herself of her last secret, whatever it was. And he would have to hear it—even if it was something dreadful, like she was in love with another man.

Carmen waited for Peter.

She waited while she listened to other guests slip from room to room, swift bars of light seen beneath her door then passing on, none of them stopping, no soft knock at her own door. Her own candles were growing shorter, and she had changed from her gown into a sensible nightrail and velvet wrapper.

She took Isabella's pearl-framed miniature from her jewel case, and laid it out carefully beside two glasses of wine.

Finally, as the small ormolu clock on the mantel chimed three, she knew that if she did not go to Peter herself and tell him the truth, she would lose all her courage. So she drank both glasses of wine herself, tucked the miniature into the pocket of her wrapper, and went to seek him out. She only prayed she would not have an awkward encounter with another guest seeking a rendezvous in the corridor!

At his door, she knocked softly, the light cast by her candle wavering as her hand trembled. "Peter?" she whispered. "It is Carmen. Are you asleep?"

There was a long silence on the other side of the door. She almost began to think he *had* fallen asleep. Then a low voice called, "The door is not locked."

She slid quickly inside the room, shutting the door carefully behind her. There were no candles lit, and the room was deep in shadows. So deep that at first her eyes could not make out anything; then she saw him, seated beside the dying fire. He was still dressed, having only removed his coat and loosened his cravat. A half-empty bottle of brandy was on the small table beside him.

Good, thought Carmen. Perhaps if they were both mildly foxed it would be easier to say what she must.

"I was just getting ready to come to you," he said. "I wanted to wait until the house settled."

"Yes. It would never do for the Earl of Clifton to cause a great scandal by slipping into his wife's room! Not the done thing at all!" said Carmen, making a weak attempt at humor. "Well, I could not wait. I had to come."

He leaned back in his chair and brought his steepled fingers to his chin. He regarded her steadily over their tips. "So, Carmen. Tell me your dreaded secrets."

She sighed. "You are not making this at all easy."

"I do apologize. Would you care for some brandy? It is excellent, some of the finest from Nick's cellar."

"Yes, please." She seated herself in the chair across from his and accepted the brandy, welcoming its calming warmth. She was suddenly very grateful for its smooth flow, for the darkness and intimacy of the room; it did seem to make painful confidences a modicum easier.

Peter leaned toward her, laid his hands lightly on her velvet covered knees. "You can tell me anything, Carmen. Surely I have proven that to you by now."

"Yes, you have."

"Then, if you are in love with someone else, if you wish to end our marriage . . ."

Carmen choked on her brandy. "In love with someone else!"

"Is that not what you wish to tell me?"

"Certainly not!" She reached into her pocket, quickly, before she could lose her courage, and drew out the miniature. She turned one of his hands over and pressed the ivory oval into his palm.

He turned it to the light of the fire, studying the painted image with a thoughtful frown. She hoped that the golden curls of the girl, the straight, small nose and stubborn chin, would tell him all he needed to know and her words could be kept to a minimum. She twisted her hands against the arms of her chair as the silence grew longer.

Then he looked up at her again, his face smooth and unreadable as marble. "What is this?"

She took a deep breath. "This is Isabella. My

daughter." He said nothing, only watched her. "She is six years old."

Peter looked back down at the painting. "She is— very lovely."

"Yes, she is."

"And what you are saying, I assume, is that she is mine."

Carmen bit her lip. "Yes. She is yours."

He closed his fingers tightly over his daughter's image. "Oh, Carmen."

Not certain what that could mean, she plunged on, telling him all she had longed to say for so long. "I think it happened on the night that we—we gave in to our feelings, after that kiss on the riverbank. Or perhaps on our wedding night. I did not realize until, well, until everything had happened and I was on my way back to Seville. I thought at first that I was ill from grief. Isabella was very tenacious to survive so much before she was even born! She stayed with me when I ran about the countryside, wounded and ill, hiding with friendly families and in gypsy camps." She paused, uncertain now what to say, what to tell next.

Without looking at her, Peter whispered, "Tell me more."

"She was born a bit early," Carmen continued, lost in her own bittersweet memories. "She was so very small. Esperanza, my old duenna, thought she would not live. She sent for the priest. But I knew, when I held her in my arms, that my girl would live and be strong. She *was* very small, but she was fierce, a true warrior; she would wave her little fists in the air both night and day, never silent. It was as if she knew what she faced, and she was fighting to live. I knew then that she was like you, with a will of iron, and that she would be fine."

A small smile touched Peter's lips. "A true Everdean."

"Oh, yes! She is very much your daughter, so stubborn, so certain of her own mind. But she is so very sweet and loving, so full of laughter. We have a grand time together." She paused. "When I thought you were dead, I wanted nothing more than to die myself. I thought I could never enjoy my life again. Isabella changed all that. She was a part of you, a gift from you, and that gave me the will to live on. Eventually I did come to enjoy my life, to appreciate a fine day, a ride on a good horse, a dance. That is entirely thanks to Isabella."

Suddenly exhausted, Carmen fell back onto her chair, trembling with emotion at all she had poured forth. Despite any lingering apprehension, she felt a very deep sense of relief. Peter knew everything, at last. Now, whatever was meant to happen could happen.

"For God's sake, Carmen!" Peter suddenly snapped. "I have a *daughter*. Why did you not tell me this sooner? Why did you not tell me the very instant we met again?"

Carmen laughed bitterly. "At the Dacey ball, you mean? And when should I have announced that we have a child together? When you were shaking me? Or when I slapped your face?"

Peter grimaced. "*Touché*, my dear. Yes, I was quite overcome with shock and anger when I first saw you again. But after we had come to an understanding, you could have told me at any time. This is so very enormous—why did you wait until now? You could have told me that day in my library."

"Elizabeth and Nicholas interrupted us, and . . ." Carmen broke off, shaking her head. "No, that is a mere excuse. I should have said something earlier, I know. I was frightened."

"Frightened? Of me?"

"You needn't look so incredulous, *querido*. You can be very intimidating, you know!"

He laughed reluctantly. "I suppose I deserve that."

"Indeed you do! And even though things appeared to be mended between us—well, disaster has come upon us unexpectedly before. Isabella was too important to risk." She reached for the bottle and poured herself another measure of brandy, taking a comforting amber swallow before she continued. "I swore to her on the day that she was born that I would always protect her, that she would never face the things I had seen. I was not certain of what you might do when you learned of her existence. You could have married Lady Deidra, and taken Isabella away to be raised by her, and I could have done little about it! Children, after all, legally belong to their fathers only. I could not risk that."

"Ah. What a sad pair we are, Carmen. I doubt even lovers in romantic novels could have been as wrapped up in half-truths and self-deceits as we have been." He held out his hand to her, and she slowly slid hers into its warmth. His fingers closed over hers. "Do you not know by now, my darling, that I could never, from the day I found you again, have wed Lady Deidra? Or indeed anyone else?"

"If it is because of our wedding, I am sure an annulment would be easy to obtain for a Catholic ceremony . . ."

His other hand came up, one finger pressed to her lips to stop the flow of words. "It is because I love you. There has never been another woman like you in the history of the world, I am sure, and no other could ever tolerate me." He grinned at her crookedly.

Carmen very much feared she would soon start crying again, and she had no handkerchief at hand.

She reached up and moved his finger from her lips. "Do you truly mean that? Do you still love me?"

"I do."

Carmen kissed his hand gently and disentangled herself from his grasp. She rose and went to the window, leaning her cheek against the cool glass. Below her, the garden slept all silvery beneath the moon, an ocean of peace.

And, at last, her own heart knew just such a perfect tranquility.

"I love you, too," she answered. "I always have."

He came up behind her. "Then, you will marry me again? At Clifton Manor, in front of all our friends and our daughter?"

Carmen closed her eyes and thought. She loved the Peter she had married six years ago, and she knew that now she loved the man he had become. As complicated and maddening as he could be! She wanted to quarrel with him and misunderstand him and kiss him until they were ninety and surrounded by grandchildren.

She turned to face him. "Yes. I will marry you again."

"Carmen!" In one step he had her in his arms, held against him so tightly that her feet left the carpet entirely. She buried her face in the silk of his golden hair and laughed aloud.

"We *will* be happy now," he said fiercely. "As we should have been all these years."

"So you are *willing* happiness on us now?"

"I am. I believe we are richly deserving of it."

"I believe you are right! But I have dreamed of this moment so many times, only to have it vanish in the daylight. What if this is a dream?"

He lowered her slowly to her feet. His hands came up to gently cradle the back of her head, his fingers in the soft curls. "My darling. Does this feel like a dream?" And he kissed her, his lips warm and soft on hers, as gentle as a spring day.

Carmen sighed and smiled as he lifted his head to look down at her. "It feels like heaven."

"I want to meet Isabella. Soon."

"Of course. I will write to Esperanza tomorrow and ask her to bring her here. Isabella will be ecstatic to come and see Elizabeth, and she will *adore* you, I am sure."

"And I will surely adore her." He laid his cheek against her hair and hugged her close. "Ah, Carmen, I can scarce fathom it! I am a father; I have a child, a daughter."

"One who is the very image of you—tall, golden, and stubborn as a bull! I cannot wait for you to meet." Carmen rested her head on Peter's shoulder, listening to the soft, ocean-wave sound of his breathing through the thin linen of his shirt.

She was sure she could feel the stirrings of some long-buried emotion—joy.

Chapter Sixteen

"Carmen! Is it really true?" The door to the library flew open, and Elizabeth rushed in, the fringed ends of her shawl swinging.

Carmen looked up from the letter she was writing, and smiled a radiant welcome. All the world seemed gloriously sunlit to her that morning, despite the fact that it was raining outside. "Is what true?"

"Come now, do not tease me! I was just talking with my brother. Are you going to be my 'official' sister?"

Carmen giggled like a schoolgirl. "It is true—sister."

"Oh!" Elizabeth threw her arms about her 'sister.' "I simply knew how it would be! I knew it would all work out beautifully, and so it has. Nick told me not to fly into the boughs, that the two of you had been apart so long that perhaps you no longer wished to be married. I said that was fustian, that of course you wanted to be married! And you do!"

"Yes," Carmen interrupted happily. "We talked all last night, and everything is settled between us."

"I am glad. I would so much rather have *you* for a sister than that Lady Deidra Clearbridge! I never had a happier hour than when she went back to London. But only think what a dash you and I will cut together in Society! And now you *must* let me paint your portrait."

Carmen laughed. Surely life would never be dull

with such a sister and brother-in-law as Elizabeth and Nicholas! "Indeed I shall! But not yet. We have a wedding to plan. And you are not to say a word to anyone yet. Peter wishes to wait to make an announcement until after he has met Isabella."

"I will be silent as tombs. Except to Nick." Elizabeth's expression turned suddenly serious. "Peter does know about Isabella, then? That she is his child?"

"Oh, yes. I told him last night."

"And was there a row?"

"Not at all. It was all much—simpler than I had supposed. He was a bit angry at first, to be sure. But I think that the happiness of the news quite overcame his anger. He is most eager to meet his new daughter."

"Well," Elizabeth breathed. "No tantrum. My brother must be maturing."

"I believe so!"

"When is he to meet Isabella?"

"That is what I wished to speak with you about." Carmen held up the letter she was writing. "I am writing to Esperanza, asking her to bring Isabella here for a few days. I thought perhaps it would be easier for her and for Peter to meet here in the country, where it is quiet and they can talk, rather than in Town."

"Yes, quite right."

"Of course, that means we must impose on your hospitality for a few days longer. Esperanza could not possibly arrive here before the end of your party. I know you have your work to return to . . ."

Elizabeth waved away her apologies. "Not at all! Nick and I were planning to stay here until next month. I am sure he will be delighted to have you and Peter and Isabella with us. And, of course, you must visit Clifton when you are so near."

"That is so kind of you, Lizzie."

"Nonsense! It will be great fun. A family holiday."
Elizabeth gathered up her shawl and prepared to depart. "This afternoon Georgina and I are going up to the attics to look for costumes. The former owners left simply piles of trunks and boxes! You must join us."

"That sounds delightful! I will see you later, Lizzie." Carmen waved to Elizabeth as she left the room, then turned back to seal and address her letter to Esperanza.

As she did so, she thought of the blackmailing letters she had tucked away in the bottom of her trunk, the ones sealed in black wax. She still had not found their writer, and that fact cast the one dark pall over her new happiness. She was always waiting for another missive to be delivered, for the sword of Damocles to drop on her head and all to be revealed to the scandal-loving *ton*.

A scandal, always to be avoided, was unthinkable now that she was soon to be presented as the Countess of Clifton, with her daughter the child of an English earl. Carmen could never bear to bring disgrace on Peter's head, of harming his promising political career and the name of his family.

She had, in her mind, ruled out Robert Means as the culprit. But if not him, then who?

The attics of Evanstone Park were not as Carmen remembered the attics at her home in Seville—dark, dusty, musty. They were wide and clean, with the smell of new wood and polish, lined with trunks left by the former owners, as well as a few that had belonged to Elizabeth's mother and grandmother.

Carmen, Elizabeth, and Georgina dug through this bounty, spreading silks, satins, and velvets across the floor in search of suitable costumes for the tableaux.

Georgina held up an elaborate gown of bright blue taffeta, its silk flower-trimmed skirts spreading wide in the style of the last century. "What do you think, ladies? Would this be quite suitable for Hera, descending from the heavens like a great bluebell?"

Elizabeth laughed and swirled a velvet cloak over her shoulders. "I like this one! I shall sweep onstage, covered from head to toe. Then I shall drop the cloak and reveal, hmm . . ." She pulled out a transparent chemise. "This! *Et voila!*"

"*Quel scandale!*" Georgina cried. She fanned herself with a large painted silk fan. "I declare I shall swoon from the shock. No vouchers for you!"

Elizabeth pushed her playfully. "You were never shocked in all your life, Georgie Beaumont! Remember that costume ball in Venice, where you wore a lady pirate gown with a skirt that ended quite at your knees?"

"I never!" Georgina gasped.

Carmen laughed at their antics, then turned back to the trunk she was excavating. It must have belonged to Elizabeth's mother rather than her grandmother, for it contained clothes of a slightly more recent vintage. And it seemed that Elizabeth's mother had been dashing indeed.

She took out a long, shimmering, one-shouldered column of silver tissue. It was almost of the right length on Carmen, and quite appropriately classical in appearance.

She held it up to her and examined the effect in the tall mirror set up in the corner.

It was beautiful, almost like a fall of liquid silver, flowing and sparkling.

She wondered what Peter would think, if he saw her in it.

She smiled softly.

Elizabeth came up beside her, to touch the magical

fabric gently with her small hand. "My mother wore this to a masquerade ball when I was a small child," she said. "It was even before she married Peter's father. I remember watching her dress for the ball. She wore a mask of white feathers and long diamond earrings. I thought her such a magical creature in it, all gold and silver. Almost like a swan!"

"Oh." Carmen held the gown away from her. "Then, I must not wear it, not if it was a very special gown of your mother's."

"No, you *must* wear it, for that very reason. It should not be hidden away in a trunk forever." She smiled mischievously. "And just imagine the look on my brother's face when he sees you in it!"

Carmen laughed. "I was thinking that very thing!"

"Then, you will wear it?"

"Yes, of course."

"Excellent! Now, I am very thirsty. Digging about in dusty old trunks is tiring work."

Carmen carefully folded the gown and laid it aside. "I will go downstairs, then, and see about some tea and cakes."

As she went down the stairs, brushing dust from her hair, she caught a glimpse of Peter as he went into the conservatory. Tucked beneath his arm was a large, colorful book of children's fairy tales.

By noon, the morning's rain had paused, bringing out azure skies and glorious sunshine. So Elizabeth's luncheon moved out to tables set up on the terrace, where guests could look at the dew-damp gardens and chatter freely about their tableaux and the cards planned for that evening.

Carmen had only just finished the dessert, when a footman came to her and spoke quietly in her ear.

"I beg your pardon, my lady," he said. "A lady has arrived who is asking for you."

Carmen looked up at him, startled. A guest, for her? "Are you certain she is not looking for Lady Elizabeth?"

"Oh, no. She said most specifically the Condesa de Santiago. I have placed them in the library."

"Them?"

"Yes, my lady. She has a child with her."

Isabella. It had to be. Carmen quickly excused herself to her table companions, and followed the footman to the library, trying to still the trepidation in her heart.

As she stepped into the dim library, a small bundle of velvet cloak and satin hair ribbons flew across the room and hurled itself at her. Small arms flung about her waist, nearly pulling her off balance.

"Mama!" Isabella cried. "Mama, Mama, I've missed you so, so much!"

"Darling Bella!" For a glorious moment the bright joy of reunion overcame any misgivings. Carmen picked Isabella up and twirled her about until the little girl squealed with laughter. She kissed her daughter's small pink cheeks over and over, and nuzzled her nose into warm golden curls. "Um, you smell of roses and rain!"

"And you smell of Mama," Isabella giggled. "Are you happy to see us?"

Carmen glanced at Esperanza, who stood by the fire wrapped in her black traveling cloak. "I am happier than happy, dearest. And I know that Elizabeth and Nicholas will be happy to see you again. But I am surprised; you cannot possibly have received my letter, as I posted it only this morning."

"Letter?" said Esperanza. "No, Carmencita, we received no letter. I just thought it best to come to you, as Isabella has been ill."

"Ill!" Carmen framed her child's face in her hands and peered into it closely, searching for any sign of dreaded illness. Isabella's complexion was all pink and white, her dark eyes clear and bright. She *was* a bit flushed, but that could be attributed to the excitement of travel. Carmen laid the back of her hand against Isabella's brow; it was cool. "She looks well. What was amiss?"

"She is well now," Esperanza replied. "But only two days ago she was quite feverish and calling for you. I thought it best to bring her to you. If only you had been at home, where you belong . . ."

"Yes," Carmen interrupted firmly. "Just so. But you were right to bring her here."

"It was only a stomachache," Isabella said, her six-year-old voice quite as scornful as her father's. Then she leaned against her mother and whispered, "I wanted *you*, Mama, because you never make me swallow awful medicines when I'm ill, as Esperanza does. You tell better bedside stories, too."

Carmen laughed. "Well, I am happy my little imp is feeling better. I am also happy that you've come to me; I have a grand surprise for you!"

"A surprise? Really? What is it? A pony?"

"Better! But you shall have to wait and see. If I told you what it is, it would not be a surprise any longer."

Isabella made a moue. "Oh, all right! I can wait."

"Good girl! Now, you wait here while I go fetch Elizabeth. She can find you the very prettiest room and make sure you are settled while I talk to Esperanza . . ."

Elizabeth, as if conjured by the mention of her name, opened the door and poked her dark head inside. "Did I hear James say your maid was here, Carmen?"

"Yes. Esperanza has brought Isabella for a visit."

"Hello, Lady Elizabeth!" Isabella cried, running

forward to give her the same exuberant welcome she had given Carmen. "I have come to see you!"

"So I see!" Elizabeth kissed Isabella's cheek. "I shall have to tell Nick what a very charming guest has come to grace our house!"

"Can we go see him now?" asked Isabella.

"Well, I . . ." Elizabeth glanced questioningly at Carmen. At her nod she took Isabella's hand and led her out of the room. "Of course, dear. Then we will find you a chamber that suits so that your mother can talk with Esperanza."

Carmen closed the library door behind Elizabeth and Isabella, and leaned back against it. "Now, Esperanza," she said. "I wish to know what really happened."

"What really happened, Carmencita?" Esperanza sank down onto a chair, her lined features weary in the firelight. "Isabella was ill, she wanted her mother. It was a stomachache, as she sometimes gets, but I thought it best to bring her to you."

"She was probably eating too many lemon drops again. But why did you not send a messenger? I would have come back to London straight away. There was no need for you to make such a journey." Carmen went and sat on the arm of Esperanza's chair, taking her duenna's wrinkled hand in hers. "Did something else, of a more alarming nature, occur after I left?"

"Alarming, Carmencita? Such as what?"

"I do not know. A message, perhaps, or an odd visitor. A break-in. Did someone follow you while you were out shopping or walking in the park?"

Esperanza shook her head. "Oh, no, *niña*. Nothing of the sort. I only thought that Isabella would be better off with her mother."

Carmen was still uneasy. It was really not at all like Esperanza to act on impulse; she had spent almost six years following Carmen's travels stoically from city to city, but she had never enjoyed it. She had always wanted predictability, such as she had had with Carmen's mother.

Something *must* have happened in Town. But Esperanza's head was almost drooping with fatigue, and Carmen did not have the heart to press her. There would be time enough for talk later.

"I am sorry, Esperanza dear," she said. "You must be so tired from your journey. Let me see you settled, then later you and Isabella and I shall have tea together, and I will tell you all of what I have been doing here. And you must tell me what you and Isabella have been up to!"

"Yes." Esperanza allowed Carmen to help her to her feet, leaning heavily on her younger arm. "Yes. Yes, I am very tired."

What the devil was detaining Carmen?

Peter glanced at his watch. She had promised to meet him for a walk in the gardens, now that the rain had ceased.

But there was no sign of her: not in the drawing room, where small groups were preparing their tableaux for Sunday evening, not in the dining room, where an afternoon buffet was set. She was not even with Elizabeth and Georgina Beaumont, who were once again foraging for costumes in the attics.

He finally decided to wait for her in the library, where he was at least assured of quiet and a good fire. He borrowed a bottle of Nicholas's best claret and a book, and settled down to have a read until Carmen chose to show herself.

He had no sooner begun the first chapter, when he was distracted by a faint but persistent hissing noise. He glanced up and saw nothing. He wondered what Nicholas was putting in his claret these days, to cause people to hear things.

"Psst! Psst!"

There it was again, assuredly *not* a figment of the claret bottle. In point of fact, he believed it to be coming from beneath his very chair.

Peter looked down and saw a white lace flounce against the deep green carpet. There was also the tip of a tiny kid slipper.

It was far too small to belong to any of the female guests, even Miss Dixon, who prided herself on her very tiny hands and feet. So he knew he was not interrupting some bizarre tryst under the library furniture. One of the servant's children, perhaps?

"Oh, my," he said. "I do believe this library is haunted."

There was a giggle.

"I sincerely hope they are friendly ghosts."

"It is not a *ghost*," a small voice said. "It is I!"

"And who might I be?"

A head popped from beneath the chair. Peter leaned over to peer at the little porcelain face framed by a tangle of golden curls and untied pink hair ribbons.

He nearly fell from his chair.

He drew back from the sight of her. "Who—who are you, child?" he whispered. Though he did not have to ask—he knew. No one else but Carmen could possibly have a daughter with such eyes, chocolate dark and slightly tilted at the corners, full of laughter and mischief.

"I am Isabella."

Peter felt a pressure against his leg, and opened his eyes to see that she had emerged from beneath the chair and was now leaning against him. Her eyes were wide and curious as she looked up at him.

"Well," he said. "How do you, Miss Isabella. It is my very great honor to meet you."

"You did not introduce *yourself!*"

"Did I not? How very remiss of me. I am Peter Everdean."

Isabella held out one tiny, dusty hand. "How do you do."

Peter took her hand and raised it to his lips.

She giggled, then completely shocked him by clambering up into his lap. She was tall for her age, but as thin and delicate as a bird as she settled against his chest. Quite as if she had been sitting there all her life.

Peter was startled and, for one of the very rare times in his life, uncertain. He had never been around children, not since he himself had been a child, and had no idea of what the proper thing to do was in such a situation.

"Well, Miss Isabella," he said, "do you always greet strangers by climbing into their laps?"

"Oh, no," she answered blithely. "Never. That awful old Comte de Molyneux in Paris wanted me to hug him when he came to take Mama to a ball, but I wouldn't let him. He smelled vile, like onions. But you smell nice." She cuddled closer. "You must be a very nice man, not like the comte."

"No. Not like the comte," he said with a laugh. Then he carefully, tentatively, put his arm around her.

That was probably proper. After all, she was his daughter.

"Yes," she announced. "I do like you, Mr. Everdean."

What a quick judge she was. "Thank you, Miss Isabella. I quite like you, as well."

"Good. Then, you will not tell anyone I am here, will you?"

Peter could feel the twist as she turned her little finger. Yes, he was well and truly caught. "Are you meant to be someplace else?"

"Oh, yes. I am meant to be napping where Lady Elizabeth put me, so Mama and Esperanza can talk. But I am not tired! I wanted to see who was at the party."

"Well," he said consideringly. "I suppose we needn't tell your mama where you are, just yet. But won't she worry?"

"Oh, no. She and Esperanza are still talking. I know because I listened at the door." Her golden head drooped against his shoulder. "And you see, I am not at all sleepy . . ."

Chapter Seventeen

Carmen had settled Esperanza in the small dressing room adjoining her own bedchamber, and had stayed with her for over an hour. Esperanza had seemed quite exhausted, pale and drawn; Carmen wondered if perhaps it was *she* who had been ill and not Isabella. She at last managed to persuade Esperanza to take some tea and lie down for a rest.

Then she went off in search of Isabella. But the little girl was not in the bedroom where Elizabeth had left her, ostensibly napping. Nor was she in the long gallery looking at Elizabeth's paintings or in the drawing room or conservatory. Carmen even ventured into the kitchen, much to the shock of the chef and kitchen maids, hoping Isabella might have gone in search of sweets. But no sign of her was found.

Then Carmen went into the library, the last place she had to look before the attics. The large wood-paneled room was absolutely quiet, dim in the very late afternoon light. The fire had burned low, and no one had been in to light the candles yet.

She was backing out of the room when she saw the hint of golden hair above the top of an armchair drawn up before the fire. She tiptoed in closer.

And almost choked on a half sob, half laughter at the sight that greeted her. Her husband was asleep in the chair, with their daughter, also sleeping, leaning against his shoulder. Isabella's tiny mouth was open against the fine blue wool of his coat, and one little hand was curled in his cravat, hopelessly mangling the once pristine folds.

Carmen pinched her own arm to be certain she was not having one of the dreams that had so plagued her over the years. Dreams where she had seen the three of them together, sitting close beside their own fire. She had always awoke to a cold loneliness, an empty bed.

A small sound must have escaped her, for Peter's eyes opened and he looked up at her. He smiled slowly.

"Am I dreaming, Carmen?" he murmured.

"I thought the same thing," she whispered. "I see you have made Isabella's acquaintance."

"Oh, yes. The imp was hiding beneath my chair, trying to avoid a nap." Peter shifted in his chair. Isabella's head lolled a bit, but she did not wake. "She is rather more weighty than she appears."

"She gets heavier when she is asleep. But that is the only time she is quiet." Carmen sat down in the chair next to his. "Shall I take her?"

"No, no. I have six years to make up for. She is so very beautiful, Carmen." He looked down at his daughter's sleeping face. "So very beautiful."

"The most beautiful girl in the world."

"She looks very much like you."

"Not at all! She looks like you."

They sat quietly together while the shadows lengthened on the floor, the only sounds the soft breaths Isabella drew in her sleep. It grew a bit chilled as the fire died away, but Carmen did not feel cold even in the thin muslin of her gown. Indeed, she had never felt warmer in all her life.

"We will have to go change for supper soon," she said at last when the sounds of people leaving the drawing room could be heard.

"Yes, of course. And the little one should be in her bed." He stood slowly, careful not to jostle the child in his arms. Isabella murmured a little and twined her arms about his neck.

"Not sleepy," she muttered, then fell back to snoring against him.

"Shall I take her to her nursery?" said Peter.

"I will go with you. Elizabeth put her in the floral chamber, just down from mine." Carmen went ahead to open the library door.

Peter kissed her cheek as he went past her. "Thank you, Carmen," he said.

"Thank you for what?"

"For giving me Isabella. For being here again."

"You are very welcome, *querido*. And this time we will not be parted again!"

"Never. I promise you that."

"I will hold you to that promise."

Isabella did not even wake when her father placed her on her small bed, removed her slippers, and drew the bedclothes about her snugly. Carmen tucked her favorite doll next to her, and kissed the top of her tumbled curls.

"Will she sleep the night through?" Peter whispered.

"Of course! She is not an infant. But if she cries out, the maid Elizabeth sent up will hear her. We really should go now, or we shall be too late."

"Yes, certainly." With a last glance at his daughter, Peter offered Carmen his arm and escorted her to the door of her own chamber. "Will you walk with me in the gardens after supper, for a quiet talk?"

"I would love nothing more. Well—*almost* nothing more!" She made certain no one was hanging about in the corridor, then kissed him lingeringly. When his arms reached out to draw her closer, she pulled away with a laugh. "Remember supper!"

"Bother supper! I am not hungry for *food*," he muttered, and reached for her again.

Carmen ducked under his arm into her room and closed the door on him. "Supper!" she called.

He protested, but soon she heard his footsteps move away down the corridor.

There was no time to ring for a maid, so Carmen quickly chose an evening gown that required small effort, a lilac satin that buttoned up the side of the low-cut bodice with tiny pearl buttons. It was only after she had pulled it on that she noticed one of the buttons was hanging on only by a thread, and her white silk chemise could be seen through the gap.

"Oh, bother!" she cried. "I will never make it to supper until the dessert." She pattered in her stockinged feet to Esperanza's dressing room chamber, intending to ask her to sew up the button.

But Esperanza was not there. The bedclothes were rumpled, and candles were lit on the dressing table, yet no one was there.

Carmen went quickly to the dressing table where Esperanza's valise was placed, intending to find a needle and make the repair herself.

What she found there was far more shocking than needles and cotton.

In the valise, beneath carefully folded shawls and caps, was a small wooden box. But instead of the sewing paraphernalia that Carmen expected to find, there was a small sheaf of cheap stationery, a clutch of pencils, a wax jack, and a few sticks of wax.

Black wax. Carmen knew for certain that Esperanza's usual wax, used to seal all her letters, was red.

A knot of ice formed in her stomach, freezing all the delicious anticipation of the evening, all the warm *life* she had begun to feel again. As she opened the jack to look at the little bits of ominous black wax still inside, the woman she had been during the war seemed to take her over again. Calm, calculating, removed from the horrible things that were really happening around her. That distance had always served her so well through war and widowhood.

Through betrayal.

But Esperanza had been with her since she was born! She had been Carmen's mother's duenna, her own companion through her terrible first marriage, through the birth of Isabella, and all her wanderings. How could she have written those letters, those ugly letters?

Carmen had suspected Robert Means, when all along it had been her own Esperanza!

She sank down onto the dressing table stool, her knees suddenly like water. She had seen betrayal before, of course, had seen hatred and rage. Yet this was a woman she had shared her life with, had let her near her own child.

It was all so awful, so unfathomable.

Carmen threw the jack onto the floor in a flash of pain and anger, all her cold distance gone.

"Oh, Carmencita," a sad, soft voice said from the open doorway. "I am so very sorry you saw that."

Chapter Eighteen

Carmen slowly stepped backward, until she felt her hips bump against the edge of the table, and she leaned against it weakly. She knew her mouth was inelegantly agape, but somehow her mind would not connect with her jaw and tell it to close. She just stared at Esperanza, enveloped in a hazy cloud of unreality.

Esperanza looked the same tidy, efficient lady Carmen had known since childhood. Her neat black silk gown was fastened at the throat with an ivory brooch that had been a long-ago gift from Carmen's mother. The lace cap atop coiled gray braids. It was all the very same. Yet something in her faded brown eyes was very different. They were sad and calm, even a bit cool, as they regarded Carmen and her shocked face.

"Carmencita," she said quietly, moving a bit nearer. "I did not mean for it to be this way."

"It—it was you," Carmen managed to whisper. "All this time. You were the one writing those letters." She sat back down slowly, her ankles suddenly unbearably wobbling.

"Yes. When we were in Paris, I gave them to a friend who was traveling to England to post at regular intervals, so you would not suspect. Very clever of old Esperanza, *sí*?" She chuckled, but her de-

meanor remained soft and regretful. "It was careless
of me to leave these things about."

"But, Esperanza! How could you do such things?"
Carmen cried. She pounded her fists against her
satin-covered thighs, like the lost child she felt inside.
"You were like a dear aunt to me, even like a mother
after Mama died. Why do you hate me so?"

"Carmencita, I *love* you! That is why I did this."

"No. Those letters were full of hatred. No one who
loved me could have written them. If you needed
money, you know I would have given you
anything . . ."

"Do you not see, *querida*? I did not do this for
money. I had to save you and Isabella from your-
selves."

Carmen stared at Esperanza, utterly aghast that she
had been so blind to such madness for so long. It
had been beneath her very roof, and she had not
seen it. Slowly, she held out one hand to Esperanza,
trembling so much that the emerald on her finger
flashed and danced merrily.

"Esperanza," she said slowly, forcing herself to remain placid and quiet as she once had with battle-
mad soldiers. "You are not at all yourself. You are
tired from all our travels, I know, and that is all my
fault. You must have rest, a permanent home. Let me
help you . . ."

"No!" Esperanza suddenly cried. She moved
closer, her fists in their innocuous black lace mitts
opening and closing against her skirts. "It was *you*
who were not yourself, Carmencita! That is why I
did what I did. To make you see. I could find no
other way."

Carmen shook her head, bewildered. She was still
reeling; she longed to scream, to cry. Instead, she
stayed very still. "Tell me, then, Esperanza. Tell me
what I must see."

"That you have not lived your life in a way that your sainted mama and the Blessed Virgin would deem proper. That you must repent and change before it is too late."

"Not proper?"

"No. In Spain, during the war, your mother and I knew that you were not with the Santiago family in Toledo, as you claimed. We knew what you were really about, riding around the countryside, associating with peasants and with English soldiers." Esperanza practically spat those words out, making "English" sound the vilest curse. "You were messing about in war and politics, as no proper woman should. I knew you were caught in evil when you came home heavy with child and with no husband. And when you had not given your lawful Spanish husband an heir as you should have!"

Carmen pressed her fist against her mouth. She felt horribly like a chastened schoolgirl, awaiting some dreadful punishment from the Mother Superior. "I told you my husband had died!"

"What husband? I saw no marriage lines!"

"Esperanza, please . . ."

Esperanza continued, unhearing. "I knew when I saw Isabella that *she* could be saved, if only you could be brought to see how wrong you were. If you could be brought to repent, to send the child to a convent to be raised." She stepped up half behind Carmen, almost concealed. "She is so like you when you were a child, Carmencita. So lovely, but so very willful. And you never discipline her as you should . . ."

Carmen closed her eyes, but she could not shut out dreadful reality. It still hung heavy about her, no dream at all. "Esperanza, please, let me help you . . ." She half rose from her stool.

The next thing she felt was a sharp, heavy pain

against the back of her head. There was a shower of light, a strange stickiness.

Then—nothing.

"I am worried about Carmen, Peter." Elizabeth tugged on her brother's coat sleeve, making him bend closer to hear her hurried whisper. She cast a quick look around at the guests gathered in the drawing room for cards after supper. "I do not wish to be a hovering hostess, but when she did not appear for supper . . ."

Peter frowned. "I am worried as well, Lizzie. It is not at all like her to not send a message if she meant to absent herself. And she said she was going to dress for supper when we parted."

"Do you think she could be ill?"

"She seemed well enough earlier. I will go and speak with her."

"Yes," Elizabeth said with a sigh of relief. "Thank you, Peter dear. I am sure all is well, and there is some easy explanation."

As Peter left the bright, chatter-filled drawing room and climbed up the dim staircase, the cold knot that had formed in his stomach as supper went on with no Carmen grew. He felt almost a sense of foreboding, an intuition that had served him well in battle.

Something was amiss with his wife.

Carmen's bedroom door was slightly ajar, a sliver of light spilling into the corridor. Wishing he had his pistol, or at least a knife, Peter slowly opened the door completely and stepped inside.

Her shawl, gloves, and fan were laid out on the bed. On the dressing table, a jewel case sat open, but, from the wealth of gems that tumbled there, he judged that nothing had been burgled. The fire had almost died away, but candles still burned brightly. The faint scent of jasmine perfume hung in the air.

It was so very quiet.

Then he heard a small sound, a rustling, coming from behind the half-closed door of the adjoining dressing room, which he knew had been made into a bedroom for Carmen's maid. Peter caught up the only weapon at hand, the fireplace poker, and went inside.

At first glance he thought the room as empty as the bedroom. Then he saw a flash of lilac satin against the floor, heard a low moan from behind the dressing table.

"Carmen!" he shouted, dropping down onto the carpet beside her prone body. Her black curls were sticky with blood, and she was alarmingly pale. For one sickening moment, he feared she was gone from him again.

But she moaned again, a bit louder, and her hand moved on the carpet.

He took that cold hand and pressed it against his chest. "Carmen?" he said urgently. "Can you hear me, love?"

"Peter?" She tried to turn her head and cried out.

"Do not move," he said. "Just try to lie still."

"Cold," she murmured.

Peter stripped off his coat and tucked it around her. "I shall have Lizzie fetch a doctor."

"Not yet! Not until . . ."

"What happened here? Can you tell me?"

Her eyes opened, unfocused and dilated until they were completely black. They darted frantically about the room. "It was Esperanza. All the time."

Peter was shocked. That frail old lady he had glimpsed earlier that day had bashed Carmen, who was a tall, athletic woman, over the head? He wondered fleetingly if Carmen was having delusions brought on by her head wound. "Your maid did this?"

"Yes!" Tears spilled down Carmen's cheeks. "She wrote all those letters. It was Esperanza all the time!" Her voice rose sharply. "I confronted her, and she hit me on the head."

He looked up at the table they were crouched behind, and saw the jumble of papers and pencils and sticks of black wax. A heavy silver candlestick, flecked with blood, was carelessly tossed there on its side.

He shuddered at the palpable sense of evil that surrounded them, as strongly as he had once felt it in battle. He carefully gathered Carmen into his arms, surrounding her with his body as if he could thus ward off anything bad from touching her. She was trembling.

"My poor dear," he whispered. "Why would she do such a thing to you?"

"I don't know!" Carmen cried. "She just went on and on about how wicked I was, how I have lived my life sinfully, and now Isabella . . ." She gasped suddenly and struggled to sit up, clawing at Peter's hands when he pressed her back down. "Isabella!"

"What is it? Did she threaten Isabella?" Peter felt such a burning rage, uncontrollable as a house fire, rising up in him. He forced himself to stay quiet as he held Carmen, to not frighten her further. "Did she?"

"I do not know! I can't remember. It is all such a jumble in my mind. But if she could do *this*, she is capable of anything!" She seized his hand, her grip painful as she pressed the bones together. "You must find Isabella, Peter. Find her, and keep her safe."

"I will, I swear. But you must stay here, and not move until a physician can get here."

"No! I must go with you . . ."

"Carmen!" Unmistakable authority rang in his voice. He pressed her gently but firmly back against the floor. "You will start to bleed again if you move about. Either you wait here for me to return, or I will not leave you."

Carmen moistened her cracked lips with the tip of her tongue, indecision flickering in her eyes. Finally she gave a small nod. "Yes."

"Good. I will not be gone long."

He kissed her on her forehead and went in search of his daughter. But in Isabella's bedroom, he found precisely what he had feared to find—nothing.

Her small bed had been slept in, the sheets turned back and rumpled. Yet they were cold, and the doll Carmen had tucked in so carefully beside their daughter was tossed to the floor. Isabella's little velvet dressing gown was still folded across the foot of the bed.

Peter picked it up, feeling the soft fabric beneath his hands; the milky-sweet little girl smell still clung to its folds. He had only just found her; how could he lose her so quickly?

"She is gone?"

He turned to see Carmen leaning weakly against the door frame, clinging to the wood to keep from falling. Her eyes were huge as she took in the empty room.

"Esperanza took her," she whispered.

"Perhaps. Or she might have simply wandered off somewhere, perhaps to find you or to look for something to drink. I do not know where her maid is, but when I find the stupid girl . . ." Carmen swayed precariously, so he swept her up into his arms and laid her on the bed before she could injure herself further. She turned her face away, weeping.

"No!" she sobbed. "Esperanza took her, I know.

She is not in her right mind! What if she does an injury to Isabella?''

Peter was quite terrified. He had never seen Carmen, his brave Carmen, so helplessly hysterical. His own fragile hold on calm was quickly slipping away. He knew that if he did not *do* something, he would soon be as frantic as Carmen and they would never find Isabella.

He sat up, drawing Major Everdean around him once again. He had a battle, the most decisive of his life, to plot.

"Carmen," he snapped. "You must cease this at once. Tell me what Esperanza said to you, if she gave you some hint as to where she would have gone."

Something in Carmen seemed to respond to the crisp authority in his voice. She sniffed and slowly sat up against the pillows. "No," she said thoughtfully. "Nothing. She said something about a convent, but there are no convents near here."

"Are you sure that was all?"

"Of course. I . . ."

"Peter! What has happened?"

Elizabeth swept into the room, holding a shrinking housemaid by the wrist. Elizabeth took in the scene of a bloodied and tearstained Carmen, a pale and grim Peter, and nodded.

"So something did happen," she said. "It was Carmen's Spanish maid?"

"How did you know?" Carmen murmured.

Elizabeth drew the maid forward. "Molly came to me with quite an odd tale. Tell them, Molly!"

"Oh, no, my lady, I can't . . ." The maid was obviously terrified, afeard she had done something wrong and was probably about to be dismissed.

"It is quite all right, Molly," Elizabeth urged. "This is terribly important. Do you not want to help that little girl?"

"Oh, yes, my lady!"

"Then, go on, please, Molly," Peter urged.

"Well, my lord, I was up here putting the bed warmers in the guest rooms, see, when I heard a bit of a set-too."

"A set-too?"

"Yes, my lord. Loud, like. Then I heard the young lady crying and saying, 'No, no.' So I came out into the corridor, and I saw the old lady. I beg pardon, your maid, Condesa. She was carrying the young lady off down the stairs, but she didn't want to go."

"The child did not?" Peter asked.

"Yes, the young lady." Molly was warming to her tale. "She tried to get away. I heard her call for her mama."

Carmen gave a choked cry.

Molly went on. "I knew this wasn't right, so I followed at a bit of a distance to see where they went."

"You were not seen?" Peter asked.

"Oh, no, my lord. I saw them go out the back doors, to the garden, and across the way to those trees. I daren't leave the house, my lord, without the butler knowing. So I told him what I seen."

"When was this, Molly?"

"Oh, my lord, 'bout an hour ago, I'd say."

"Damn!" Peter raked trembling fingers through his hair. "They could be anywhere by now."

Carmen reached for his hand. "We must make up a search party, quickly."

"Of course. Lizzie, will you help me?"

"I will go down now and tell Nick to have some horses readied." She started to turn away, then snapped her fingers. "The ruins?"

Peter looked at her sharply. "What ruins?"

"That old medieval tower, of course!" Elizabeth said, excited. "You follow the path through those trees to get to the tower on foot, remember? The butler does like to brag of the local sights to guests. Perhaps he told Esperanza of the tower, and she thought it a fine hiding place."

"Surely that is where they have gone!" said Carmen. "Esperanza is fascinated by romantic old ruins; they are the only things she has enjoyed on our travels. And it is beginning to rain, so I am sure they will have sought shelter."

"I will go there at once," Peter answered. "Lizzie, tell Nick and Viscount Huntington to come after me, but quietly. There must be no charging ahead full force like some cavalry, not when dealing with so unhinged a person."

"Of course, at once." Elizabeth hurried away, pulling the now-grinning maid behind her.

"I will come with you," Carmen announced.

"No!" Peter said firmly. "There is no knowing what will be found, Carmen. If something terrible has happened, or if I am forced to take some drastic action . . ."

"Do you think I have no stomach for whatever might happen?" She grasped his arm and forced him to look at her. She was pale as snow, her eyes huge and dark, but she was utterly composed now. Her earlier hysterics were gone, and in her face could be seen only steely resolve.

"Peter," she said, "you know the horrible things I have seen in my life, and that I have always done what was necessary, without flinching."

He nodded slowly. "Indeed you did. You were the best shot I have ever seen."

"Then, take me with you now! I will go whether you say aye or nay, but we would be so much more effective if we work together." Her grip tightened. "She is my *child*. I cannot sit here idly while she is in danger. After all is finished, I promise I will rest and see the doctor, and whatever else you like."

Peter sighed, resigned. "Very well. But put on a cloak! It is cold and wet outside."

She smiled faintly. "Of course, Major."

"Carmen . . ."

"Yes?"

"We will find her." His voice was implacable, yet somehow searching for reassurance.

"Oh, yes. We must."

The alternative was completely unthinkable.

Chapter Nineteen

It was a misty night, foggy and damp, not at all like the night they had their midnight picnic. The moon was almost completely obscured by clouds, casting the landscape into a dangerous darkness. Carmen and Peter had been forced to leave their horses and proceed down the narrow path on foot. They kept the lantern they had brought shuttered, so as not to reveal their progress. The only saving grace was that it had not yet begun to rain in earnest, just spitting little dribbles at them.

Carmen marveled that such a landscape, so pastoral and idyllic only days before, could look like the setting of the darkest nightmare now.

She held tightly to Peter's hand as they walked along the path. In her other hand she clutched the cold steel of her loaded pistol. As the cold air swept up her legs, she wished vaguely that there had been time to change into trousers. The thin satin of her evening gown, even covered by a heavy cloak, hardly seemed the proper armor for going into battle.

But the only thought that could stay in her mind was of Isabella. Where was she? Was she cold? Was she frightened? Did she call out for her mama?

Carmen bit her lip until she tasted blood to keep from crying out. This was not the time for panic; this was a time for cold, rational calm.

She looked at Peter and was reassured by the hard

set of his jaw, the icy light in his eyes. Here was not the English earl, who danced so gallantly in ballrooms, but the warrior she had first met. He would get their daughter back for her, no matter the obstacles. She was sure of that.

"There it is," he whispered.

The trees thinned out, and the path widened, revealing the ruined tower set atop its bluff. The stream beside which Carmen and Peter had talked ran behind it, swollen now with the rain.

Peter drew his field glasses from inside his greatcoat and examined the tower. Carmen remembered that, though the stones were crumbling, the stairs that curved up the center of the tower were intact and passable. They led to a small room at the very top of the structure, where medieval warriors had kept watch for their enemies.

"Do you see anything?" she whispered.

"No. It is too confounded dark."

Yet even as they spoke, they saw a small light flicker and die, then flicker again in the windows at the top of the tower.

"Did you see that?" she hissed. "It must be them!"

"Perhaps. Or perhaps it is merely vagrants."

"We must find out."

"Yes. Remember to stay behind me at all times, Carmen. Do you understand? No matter what we may see?"

"Of course."

"Do you have your pistol?"

"Yes, loaded and ready."

"Excellent." Peter turned suddenly and pulled her into his arms for a brief, hard kiss. "Then, once more into the breach, eh, Carmen?"

"Peter . . ."

"Yes?"

"I love you."

"And I love you. After tonight, my dear, shall we strive to live the dullest lives imaginable?"

"Oh, yes, please!"

He smiled down at her, then released her to walk off across the clearing toward the tower. He looked every bit the nonchalant Englishman, off for a bit of an evening stroll, but Carmen knew that concealed beneath his stylish many-caped greatcoat was a sword and two pistols.

Praying that no one was watching their approach, Carmen followed him, her own pistol primed and ready. Despite the enveloping warmth of her fur-lined cloak, she shivered.

It was when she slipped inside the open doorway of the tower and reached for Peter's hand for assistance ascending the crumbling stairs, that she heard it. A faint cry, a rumble of low, hurried, feminine voices. There was a golden spill of light from above.

Her eyes met Peter's. "Go," she mouthed.

He nodded, and quickly, nimbly ran up the stairs, his soft-soled boots silent on the old stone. He turned a corner, and was gone from her sight.

As per their agreement, she would wait a full minute before following. The longest minute of her life.

She leaned against the cold stone wall, the chill damp seeming to seep into her very bones. She held the pistol against her side. If only this were all over, her daughter in her arms . . .

Just as she thought she could not bear to wait another instant, she heard the deeper tones of Peter's voice, echoing from above. The rising, heavily accented voice of a woman. A shrill cry, a sob.

Carmen pushed away from the wall and ran up the stairs as quickly as she could over the stones crumbling beneath her half boots. She kept one gloved hand on the slimy wall for balance.

At the top of the stairs, she did not give in to

her longing to rush headlong into the lamp-lit room. Instead, she held back to the shadows, peering around the sharp corner of the wall.

Esperanza was there. Her usually immaculate black gown was dusty and torn, her cap gone and hair straggling from its pins. She stood near the window, her back to the night. One hand held a long dagger; the other clutched Isabella's arm.

Carmen bit her lip. He daughter was shivering in only her nightrail, her tangled blonde curls falling over her shaking shoulders. She was crying, her little face pale and streaked with tears and dirt.

Peter stood just inside the doorway, his arms held out as if to show surrender. His voice was very low and soft as he spoke.

"Please, Esperanza," he said slowly. "Please, I have not come to hurt you. I have only come to take you and Isabella back to the house. It is very cold here; this is not a place for a child."

Esperanza backed up another step, pulling Isabella with her. She was now almost leaning on the low sill of the window. "No!" she cried. "You need not pretend innocence with me, *your lordship*. I know who you are."

"Who am I, Esperanza?"

"It was you who spoiled my Carmencita, my innocent girl! Who lured her into wickedness."

"I do not know what you mean." Peter's voice was soft, almost tender. He took a very small step forward, then immediately halted as Esperanza backed up, sending a shower of stones from the window to the cobbles below.

"You *do* know what I mean! You were the English soldier who seduced Carmen, encouraged her in unseemly actions when she should have been at home. I know, because you are the image of Isabella! You are this child's father! You abandoned them to sin."

"You are wrong. Carmen was, is, my wife. There was never anything sinful about it."

"So she claimed." Esperanza pulled Isabella closer against her. She was shaking as if in a hurricane gale. "You pulled Carmen down into evil, and now she is lost. Now you are trying to do the same to Isabella. But I will save her!"

"She is my daughter. I would never do anything to hurt her, Esperanza. Now, please let me take you back to the house."

Isabella stared at him with huge, bewildered dark eyes. She strained against Esperanza's grasp. "You—are my papa?"

Peter took another step toward them. Esperanza stepped back again, sending another clatter of stones below. Carmen could hear the pounding of horses' hooves, coming closer to the tower.

Esperanza obviously heard them, as well. She glanced back over her shoulder and gasped.

Carmen sensed that their time was growing short. Esperanza was perilously near the edge of the unstable window frame, and her eyes were wilder and more unfocused than ever before. Slowly, Carmen pushed back her cloak and lifted the pistol. She stepped away from the wall to take aim . . .

"Mama!" Isabella's sudden scream made Esperanza whip her head back around. Her wide, startled gaze took in Carmen and the gun.

"Demon!" Esperanza whispered.

Then Isabella tugged hard on her arm, catching Esperanza by surprise. The soles of her shoes skidded on the stone floor, and she began to lose her balance. As Carmen watched, horrified, Esperanza fell backward, toward the windowsill, her hand still gripping Isabella.

"Papa, help!" Isabella screamed, her free hand

flailing in midair as she was pulled toward the window, her bare feet dangling off the floor.

Carmen screamed as well, and rushed forward even though she knew she was much too far away to catch her in time. Her feet seemed made of lead.

Peter, though, was much closer to them. Sleek and swift as a tiger, he lunged at his daughter, and caught her small hand, pulling her back from the brink along with Esperanza.

The momentum of their weight sent him skidding backward, to land on his back with Isabella atop him. For a moment they both lay still.

Esperanza slumped on the floor near the window, sobbing.

"*Madre de Dios*," Carmen whispered. She tossed aside the pistol and fell to her knees beside her family. She could not even feel the bite of the sharp stones through the thin satin of her gown as she watched them stir. Isabella, sobbing, fell into her mother's arms.

"Sh, my darling," Carmen murmured. "It is well now. You are safe."

Across the room, Esperanza stirred, her shoulders shuddering as she took a deep, shivering breath. Carmen put Isabella into Peter's arms and went to her, crouching down at her side.

"Esperanza," she said very quietly. "Are you hurt?"

Esperanza began sobbing in earnest at the sound of her voice. Great tears fell from her wrinkled cheeks onto her dusty black skirts. She covered her face with her hands. "What have I done? What have I done?"

"Sh," Carmen said, just as she had with Isabella. She drew Esperanza carefully into her arms, cradling her against her shoulder, as Esperanza had done so often for her when she was a child. "It is quite all right now. Everyone is safe."

"No!" Esperanza lifted her head to stare frantically up at Carmen. Her twisted, thin hands clutched at Carmen's hand. "I would never have hurt Isabella, *niña*, never! You must believe me."

"I believe you. I know you would not want to hurt Isabella."

"She is like my own child, just as you were." Esperanza's grip tightened. "Just as my Isabella was."

"Yes. My mother loved you very much, Esperanza."

"As I loved her! I did this for her."

"For my mother?" Carmen still kept her voice soft and steady, despite her own bewilderment and sorrow.

"Before she went to the angels, she charged me to look after you. She said she feared you had a wild soul, that you would not live your life in a manner befitting your station. A manner the Blessed Mother would approve." Esperanza's head drooped against Carmen's shoulder, and Carmen's arms clasped closer about her. "I saw that her fears were correct when you came back to us so heavy with child, and so silent. You laid in bed all day, with your face turned to the wall, refusing to speak. You said nothing about the Englishman you claimed had been your husband. I thought your silence was shame at your disgrace."

"It was not shame. It was grief."

"I only wanted to save you, Carmencita!" Esperanza wailed. "Never harm you. You must believe me! You must!"

"I do believe you, Esperanza. Of course I believe you."

"Do you, Carmencita? Truly?"

"I do."

Then, as Esperanza subsided back into tears, Carmen became aware of other voices.

"Mama!" Isabella sobbed. She left Peter's arms and crawled onto her mother's lap, burying her face against her shoulder. She was shaking and scared, but seemed physically unharmed. "Why did Esperanza do that? Why? I was so scared!"

"My poor angel." Carmen kissed the top of Isabella's head and held her very, very tightly. "Esperanza is very ill. She did not know what she was doing or saying. But all is well now; Mama has you safe."

Isabella clutched at her cloak. "Is Peter safe, too? Is he hurt?"

Carmen looked over at Peter, who had laid back down on the stones. He seemed rather stunned by his fall, but his eyes were open and focused as he watched them, his chest rising and falling steadily.

"I don't think he's hurt, dearest," she said. "You see, he is getting up now."

Isabella watched as Peter painfully climbed to his feet, leaning against the wall. "He said he was my papa."

Carmen sighed. "Yes, darling. He is. But I shall explain it all to you tomorrow, when you are warm and rested."

Isabella, however, seemed to require no explanations just at present. She just nodded and cuddled closer to her mother. Her eyelids were drooping in exhaustion.

Peter came to them then, wincing as he tried to put his weight on his left leg. "Carmen," he murmured, "we should go."

"Yes, of course. The others should be here any moment; perhaps they have brought horses for us. You should not walk on that leg."

"I am quite all right. Here, let me have Isabella. You should see to Esperanza. I think that . . ."

Whatever he was going to say was lost in a shout from below. "Peter!" Nicholas called. "What has happened? Are you all right? Is Isabella with you?"

Peter limped to the ruined window, a sleeping Isabella against his shoulder, and peered out. "Yes, and we are all well, if a bit shaken. I think I have sprained my ankle."

"We'll be up to help you!" Nicholas answered. "Don't go anywhere!"

"Ha! This is no time for witticisms." Then Peter turned to look at his Carmen and Esperanza, huddled on the stone floor. "*Are* you well, Carmen?"

It seemed such an insane thing to say at such a moment, but he could think of nothing else. What did one say after all the people one loves most have faced death and madness? No words could possibly articulate all the vast emotions roiling inside of him. Rage, battle exhilaration, relief, hope—love.

Above all, love.

"Oh, yes. No. I am not sure." She laughed, a bit hysterically, then rose to her feet, holding Esperanza against her. Her old duenna was in a stupor now, murmuring in Spanish as she went with Carmen without a protest. "But we must go now. We must get help for Esperanza."

Nicholas came up the tower steps then, his gaze darting sharply about the room, taking in the four weary, battle-scarred figures. He went to Carmen and took the weight of Esperanza from her arm.

"*Señora*," he murmured solicitously. "Please allow me to escort you someplace warm."

Esperanza nodded vaguely and went with him without a murmur. It was painfully obvious that she was no longer at all aware of where she was. She had unburdened her heart, been granted forgiveness, and now she had retreated to someplace very far away.

Peter went to Carmen as she watched Esperanza leave with Nicholas. He wrapped his arms about her and their child, precious treasures, and tried to will warmth into them. "Do not worry now, my love. All will be well now. All will be well."

Carmen sobbed against his shoulder.

Chapter Twenty

It was late afternoon of the next day by the time Peter managed to conclude his business. With Elizabeth's help, he had seen Esperanza settled with a local woman, a former army nurse, in her cottage at Clifton. He had not had time to bathe or eat or sleep, but he went directly to Carmen's room after he returned from the woman's cottage.

She was asleep in her bed, Isabella curled against her, also deep in slumber. A dinner tray on a nearby table was mostly untouched; but Isabella sported smears of candy on her little chin and clean nightdress, so he knew they were not entirely unnourished.

Peter smiled at the lovely sight. He drew a chair to the bedside, very quietly so as not to wake them, and settled down to the very important job of watching them.

Dark purple marred the delicate skin beneath Carmen's eyes, but she seemed a trifle less pale than she had last night. The tousled black curls that fell across her brow made her appear almost as young as her daughter.

But Peter felt himself to be positively ancient. He had lived a lifetime in one night, a life of such joy and terror and pain. He had spent so many years completely alone, trapped in a hell of guilt that had been of his own making. Then there had been a miracle. He had been given a family, the one love of his life and a beautiful child. He had experienced the most glorious feeling in life, the feeling of not being alone any longer, of knowing he would never be alone again.

He had watched his sister and her husband, had seen the life they were making together, and he had been envious. He had thought he could never find a love such as they had again; it was surely a onetime only gift, and his was gone. Then he had found Carmen again, and could see a future for them that was quite as rosy as the one awaiting Elizabeth and Nicholas. He could make love to his wife, not the mechanical physical release he had known with his mistresses, but to truly lose himself in her warmth, her love. He could play and laugh with his daughter, perhaps even hold new babies in his arms. More golden little girls and a dark-haired heir.

And he had almost lost all of that, all his fragile dreams, in one shattering second.

But here they were, safe and alive.

Peter reached for Carmen's hand, the one wearing the wedding ring she had kept so faithfully all their years apart. He raised it to his lips.

"Oh, Lord," he murmured. "I know I have been a wretched pagan. I only pray that I am worthy of all these gifts You have given me."

And let our lives be peaceful and dull now, he added silently. At least for the next forty or fifty years.

Carmen stirred and blinked up at him. "Peter? Who are you talking to?"

"I am praying."

"*You?*"

"Yes, love, me."

"I do not think I have ever heard you pray before. Not even before a battle."

"I do not think I ever have. Until now."

"Why now?"

"I merely thought I should give thanks for the wonderful miracles bestowed on us. And I was humbly asking for a very dull life in our years to come; I have had quite a surfeit of adventure now."

"Amen to that! Do you think He will grant your request?"

"Hm, at least until it is time to marry Isabella off. I have the sense that that will be no easy task."

"No, indeed!" Carmen looked down fondly at her sleeping daughter. "Fortunately, we will not have to worry about it for many years yet."

"But what if we have more? What if we have six daughters, and have to deal with six betrothals?"

"God forbid!" Carmen laughed. Then her gaze turned serious as she looked at him. "Oh, Peter. How could I have made such a dreadful mistake? How could I have left my child in the care of a madwoman? We could all have been killed last night, all because I was so blind."

"How could you have known? You knew Esperanza your whole life; you trusted her. Of course you could not have believed that of an old woman. No one would have."

"I *should* have seen it!"

Peter slid onto the bed next to her, boots and all, and drew her and Isabella into the warm circle of his arms. Her hair was soft against his beard-roughened cheek, and she still smelled of jasmine even after their long night.

"My dear," he said. "You are not culpable in this. Some people are not—not *right* in their minds, for whatever reason. Esperanza is one of them. I was one when I came home from Spain. I did some dreadful things. I could not see reality, just as Esperanza could not. Does that, then, make my sister at fault, for not seeing my illness and dispatching me directly to Bedlam?"

Carmen shook her head. "Certainly not!"

"No. Certainly not. It is the same for you. Isabella is safe. We are all here, together. So we can move into the future now, free of doubt and guilt." For the first time in years, Peter himself knew that to be true.

The past was gone, and they were free.

Carmen nodded then, and turned her face up to his. There were tears in her dark eyes, sparkling like crystals, but they could not rival the brilliance of her smile.

Chapter Twenty-One

"Carmen? May I come in?"

Carmen smiled at her reflection in the dressing table mirror at the sound of her husband's voice.

Her husband. How her heart thrilled at those words, at knowing they were true at last, and not a mere futile wish.

"Come in!" she called. She rose to her feet, straightening the folds of her silver tissue gown.

"I was coming to see if you were quite prepared for this ridiculous tableau . . ." His words trailed away, and he came to an abrupt halt inside the bedroom door at the sight of her. "Carmen. You look—entrancing."

"Do you like it?" She twirled about, displaying the full effect of the gown, the laced sandals, the diamond bandeau in her hair. "I found it in Elizabeth's trunk in the attic. She said it once belonged to your stepmother."

"I am certain that Isobel, as lovely as she was, could never have looked half so beautiful in it." He came to her and took her in his arms. His kiss was warm and lingering, a healing touch, a benediction, on all they had faced and overcome.

"If you continue like this," Carmen murmured against his lips, "we will never make it to the tableaux."

"Hang the tableaux," he answered, and reached his hand toward her bodice.

She stepped back with a laugh. "Lizzie would be very vexed with us! And Isabella would be so disappointed. She is looking forward to showing you her Cupid costume."

"Then, I suppose we must not miss it," he sighed. "I do look forward to seeing our daughter attired as Cupid. She is very likely darling in it."

"Yes, she is. And, speaking of costumes, is that cloak you are muffled in yours?"

"Er, no. But I think I may keep it on."

"Oh, no! That, sir, is not allowed. You must let me see your costume. You have seen mine."

"Very well. But first close your eyes."

Carmen squeezed her eyes shut. "They are closed."

There was a rustle of cloth, another long-suffering sigh, then, "All right. You may look now."

Carmen opened her eyes. And gave a great shout of laughter.

Peter stood before her attired in a rather brief white muslin, gold trimmed tunic. His legs, muscled and dusted with fine, blond hairs, were bare from the knee down to his laced gold sandals.

His face, usually so very cool and haughty, was a bright cherry red as he tugged at the tunic's hem.

Carmen sat down on the edge of her bed, as she feared she might otherwise fall over with the force of her mirth. "Oh!" she gasped. "It—it is wondrous."

"Elizabeth made me wear it," he muttered.

"I adore it! You should dress in this fashion every day."

Isabella burst into the room, trailed by her harried new maid. She wore a miniature of her mother's gown, only made of a heavier silver satin. A crown of silver leaves perched atop her curls, and she held a tiny bow and arrow.

"Oh!" she cried. "You look *beautiful*, Mama." Then she looked at Peter. "And so do you, Papa. Though I have never seen a man's *legs* before."

Carmen buried her giggles behind her hand.

Isabella came to her mother and leaned against her happily. "What a very nice looking family we are!" she proclaimed with great satisfaction.

"Endymion the shepherd, as his flock he guarded, she the moon Selene . . ."

Isabella, perched atop a short marble column, angelic in her silver gown, faltered, and glanced uncertainly at her mother.

Carmen struggled to hold her pose without laughing. Her lovely gown was proving too thin for the rather chilly night, and goose bumps had popped out on her shoulders. Her arms ached from holding aloft her wooden, silver-painted moon. And Peter, stretched out on the floor of the makeshift stage as the sleeping shepherd, kept surreptitiously reaching out to grab her ankle.

It was the grandest fun she had had in years. So very welcome after such dreadful events.

Without turning her head, she whispered, "Selene saw him, loved him, sought him . . ."

Isabella frowned and lowered her little bow. There was actually no Cupid in the myth, but the role had been invented for her at the last moment, and she wanted to play it to the hilt. "Must I say that, Mama?" she said very loudly.

The audience laughed.

"Yes, dear," said Carmen. "It is part of the speech."

"Very well," Isabella sighed. "But since you have already said it, I don't think I ought to repeat it." She lifted her bow again. "And coming down from heaven, kissed him and lay beside him."

Carmen knelt down beside Peter and loudly kissed him on the cheek.

Isabella laughed. "You have lip rouge on your cheek, Peter!"

The audience, already warm with champagne and the general hilarity of all the tableaux (especially the one where Elizabeth, as Hera, had entered trailing twenty feet of blue velvet curtain behind her) collapsed in mirth.

Isabella faced the merrymakers with a fierce scowl on her little face. "We are not finished yet!"

Elizabeth, her own whoops concealed behind her hand, waved her fan at her guests. "Yes, do let them finish!"

Isabella nodded in satisfaction. "Evermore he slumbers, Endymion the shepherd."

There was silence.

"*Now* we are finished," she said, and jumped off her column perch to curtsy.

There was wild applause, and everyone rose from their chairs in ovation.

"Bravo!" cried Georgina, her red curls twisted wildly in her guise of Medusa. "What an actress you have here, Carmen. Bring her to Italy one day, and we shall put her on the stage at La Fenice."

Isabella's eyes widened in delight. "Really?"

Carmen swung her daughter up in her arms. She kissed her little cheek, leaving the second smudge of lip rouge of the evening. "No stage for you, dearest! But you did do a very fine job tonight, Bella."

Peter rose from the floor, tugged the rather brief skirt of his toga down again, and came to stand beside his wife and daughter. "So fine I believe it merits staying up for supper."

"Bravo!" Isabella crowed.

Carmen looked up at Peter as he took her arm.

She raised her brown eyes inquiringly. "Now do you think?" she whispered.

"Now is quite as good a time as any other. Don't you agree—Lady Clifton?"

Carmen smiled. "Once more into the breach!"

Peter faced the chattering crowd and raised his hand for their attention. A silence fell.

"My friends," he said. "I—we have a rather surprising announcement to make . . ."

Epilogue

"And I pronounce that you be man and wife. Amen."

Carmen's hand, newly adorned with a band of diamonds as well as her emerald, trembled in her bridegroom's grasp, and she was certain she was about to cry. But she blinked the tears away and smiled as she lifted her face for Peter's kiss.

A kiss that went on for so long, that the good vicar coughed in a delicate disapproval, and Elizabeth and Isabella could be heard giggling from the first pew.

Peter finally drew back and gazed down at her warmly. "Well, Carmen. Do you feel *more* married than you did ten minutes ago?"

"Not a bit. But this *is* a lovely moment. Do you feel more married?"

"No. But I did hear that Lizzie's excellent chef has prepared a lovely lemon cake, so that should make all this wedding folderol worthwhile."

"Folderol? Do you not recall that this was all *your* idea?"

"Was it? Hm. Perhaps it was." He stepped back and very politely offered his arm. "Shall we move forth, Lady Clifton?"

"Thank you, Lord Clifton. We shall."

So they processed down the aisle to the booming strains of the church organ, amid the cheers of the few good friends gathered there in the old Norman church of Clifton Village. In the sunny churchyard, they were quickly surrounded and showered with a fall of rose petals.

"Oh, Carmen!" Elizabeth cried, wiping at her eyes with her lacy handkerchief. "I have never seen a bride so lovely." She straightened the folds of Carmen's ivory-colored lace mantilla, which fell from her high comb over her simple ivory satin gown.

"I should be," Carmen said. "You and Georgina spent hours fussing over me this morning!"

"My mama is the loveliest woman in the world!" Isabella announced, leaning against her father's leg. She was quite pretty herself, in a new white dress with a pink silk sash. Even her curls were tidy for once, brushed and threaded with a wreath of pink rosebuds.

"Indeed, she is one of the loveliest women in the world," said Peter, catching his daughter up in his arms and kissing her cheek. "You and your Aunt Elizabeth are the others!"

Isabella giggled.

Elizabeth beamed. "Shall we go back to Evanstone, then? Pierre will pout so if his magnificent wedding breakfast grows cold."

"Ah, yes. The famous lemon cake. What do you say, my loves?" Peter said. "Shall you ride with us, Bella?"

"Yes!" Isabella shouted. She wriggled down from her father's arms, and ran toward the flower-bedecked open carriage that awaited them outside the churchyard gates. "Come on!" she called. "All the villagers are lined up along the road to wave to us!"

And Peter and Carmen looked at each other then ran down the pathway amid more rose petals and laughter, to join their daughter and be carried forward to their new life.